MUNCY

GARY T. BRIDEAU

MUNCY

iUniverse books may be ordered through booksellers or by contacting:

iUniverse
1663 Liberty Drive
Bloomington, IN 47403
www.iuniverse.com
844-349-9409

ISBN: 978-1-6632-5785-7 (sc)
ISBN: 978-1-6632-5791-8 (e)

Library of Congress Control Number: 2023921532

Print information available on the last page.

iUniverse rev. date: 11/27/2023

Contents

The Mysterious Stranger

The Characters in the Story

Muncy A Collans:
In this novel, she is married to John Bilmore, aged twenty-eight, height 5'6 tall, 130 Lbs. and is from the planet Pylee. She has a heart-shaped mole on her left butt cheek. She graduated college with a 4.0 average. Her favorite foods are cappuccino, Rocky Road ice cream, and Boston Cream donuts. She always plans and thinks things out before doing it and is the Tram operator at the Institute.

Steve T Rogers:
Muncy's boyfriend, who is a tyrant

JoJo:
Her full name is Joanna Josephine Joplin, and she has the agility of a cat. She is nicely built, medium-high, with short brown hair, and in her early twenties. She is friends with Connie, Kitty, and Mosey. JoJo gets into more trouble than she is worth. She had traveled ninety years in the past and almost died. In 1920, she was known as Maryanne or Future Lady.

Missy, W. **Wells**
Sprite, with light brown curly hair, is from Slandor and is thirty-four inches tall. She is Pixy's younger sister. Missy loves weird sandwiches and is in charge of the Sprite menu at the Institute. Missy is the General Supervisor of the Tram depots and the Sprite food inspector.

Tippy:
A Will-o-the-wisp, she is from Dicapl and is 6' feet tall. Her mother is Megan, and her father is Agar. She first appears in Quest, a Journey.

Where she accidentally stole Harry for a mate. She becomes Prince Blue's gal Friday because of the way she handled herself with a giant spider called a Tree Walker.

Darlene Comstock:
A well-proportioned thirty-three-inch-tall sprite with long blond hair and a friend of Mary Bell is in charge of the Institute Tram Depot.

Snow Wolf:
This creature is nearly the size of a horse with long, bone-white, shaggy hair and has massive golden eyes with three-inch long fangs. One drop of its saliva will cause the body to swell until it explodes from the pressure. During that time, the victim gasped for air and is in extreme pain.

Greg LaMore:
He is a tall, husky man in his early thirties, wearing jeans and shirts, and is a nuisance.

Kayli Aubrette:
A fisty Sprite, age 25, is twenty-eight inches tall, is from the planet Pylee, and is on the sprite security at the Institute.

Dina:
A female self-sustaining Avatar or a solid, three-dimensional computer image. She can upload herself into any internet outlet or computer. She is six feet tall with long brown wavy hair, clad in a long forest green dress, green hair with flowers.

Rose M. Stromberg:
She is married to Thor Stromburg. She wears perfume, which gives off a gentle scent of roses. She is six feet tall with long, silky brown hair and a fair complexion. She loves long flowery, pale-colored dresses. Her bright blue eyes sparkle when she speaks. She was suspended in a void for fifty years as Agar used her as his means of strength. Her parents were Carol and Josh Bud. Because of a time, warp, Rose is now married to Thor.

Thor:

Or Thor Manning Stromberg is six feet tall, has deep brown hair, and is rugged looking. He works better alone and has a tough time working in a group unless he is the leader; he can accomplish more things when he is alone and can easily focus on a task set before him. Thor grew up on a farming planet and was more trouble than he was worth because of his powerful desire for adventure. His parents did everything they could to teach him farming, to no avail. When he reached nineteen years old, Sam took him under his wing and gave him a job working for the Agency on the planet Avalon Prime. He is now in charge of the Institute, hidden on a small planetoid in an undisclosed galaxy. Thor is an independent, self-willed individual and will put his life on the line when needed. Thor loves his coffee and can drink eight cups daily without thinking about it.

Moonbeam Victoria Dakota:

A female Sprite, with yellow hair thirty-six inches tall" from the frozen tundra of Dicapl. She has extraordinary powers when she holds onto a person and can tell their emotions. She loves yellow to the point that most of her clothes are yellow. Moonbeam is head of Sprite security and is spiteful and will get even if someone planks a prank on her.

John *Bilmore*:

He is just under six feet tall, has brown hair, and spent most of his time surfing until he had to take charge of the underground complex

The Royal Blue Macaw:

Horatio is Cathy Loganberry's new invention; it's a drone designed like a bird picture below. It can be controlled by verbal command. It has a 500-terabyte memory and a video camera that can capture an ant on the ground at a thousand feet up. It collects information, and the solar collector recharges the battery in its beak.

Sam:

He is short, about five feet three inches tall, and rather plump with red hair. He lives for the adventure; the more danger involved, the better he likes it. And is called Admiral Sam the Stout.

Nicklaus Pawlet:
He is a tall man in his early thirties, wears suit pants and shirts, is helpful to Muncy, and is married to Starlight Pawlet.

Starlight Pawlet:
she is a petite woman, five feet two, with short black hair, and is very smart.

About the Galaxy Sentinel series

Thor, or The Galaxy Sentinel, is in charge of the Institute, a five-story red brick building on top of a mountain on a jungle-dominated planetoid.

The Institute is a five-story red brick building that houses the galaxy's most feared and dangerous criminals, guarded by a highly trained staff of two hundred and fifty men and women.

Thor does not work above the law; he works with the law, tracking down hardened criminals and locking them up out of society's way for good,

The law of the Planetary Alliance says that if a felon is caught committing a crime. There is no trial to determine if he is guilty; his actions are testimony against him, and he is without excuse, and a hearing is held to determine the criminal's sentence. If he is caught in the middle of committing a crime there is no long trial, because he is without an excuse.

However, if there is a shadow of doubt about whether he is guilty, there is a trial to decide his fate.

The Galaxy series consists of Leprechauns, Sprites, Will-o-the-wisps, which look like six-foot pixies, and various types of aliens. The Institute is a vast complex comprised of an Arboretum, a beach at the foot of the mountain, a large housing complex with a cafe, a large store, and a Three-Dimensional Particle Acceleration System on the fifth floor of the Institute that is far better than any hologram, and an underground tramway.

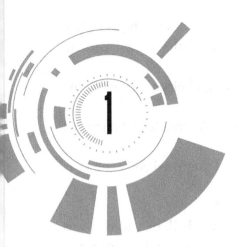

A narrow escape

Muncy Collans was dressed in jeans and a red blouse, twenty-eight years old, and is five feet six inches tall was driving back home to Wickenburg, Arizona when she felt dizzy and pulled to the side of the highway. Then muttered, "I have got to get AC in this stupid car before this heat kills me." Quickly glanced to her right and saw a man with neatly combed light brown hair clad in black pants, and a deep blue short-sleeve shirt, five-foot-six, smiling at her from the passenger seat. Thinking he would attack her, she threw her can of cola at him screaming, "Get out of my car before I call the cops and have your butt thrown in jail!"

The man stated with a pleasant smile, "My butt may wind up in the slammer, but the rest of me will still be here loving you,"

Muncy screamed, "I said get out of my car, you sorry excuse of a human."

Another wave of dizziness swept over Muncy, causing her to fall back in her seat and pass out. She came too with a highway patrol officer knocking on her window. She rolled it down, and the officer asked, "Are you alright, ma'am?"

"Yes, thank you. I closed my eyes for a bit and didn't know how tired I was, and I live just up the road,"

Muncy parked her red 1966 Ford Galaxy 500 in the driveway of her stucco ranch, picked up the cola can from the passenger's side of the car, stared at it, and thought, *I think I'm gonna switch to green tea because there may be something in these cans of cola that is making me hallucinate.*

Inside her home, Muncy sat at her shiny chrome desk in the den when her cell phone rang. She said, "City morgue, you stab them, we slab them. Hi boss, what's up,"

A man in a deep voice stated, "I hired you a helper and should be arriving at your home in about 5 minutes,"

"But boss, I told you when you hired me as a journalist, I didn't need help because they would only be in my way."

"You're taking too much on yourself, and you need someone else, like it or not,"

"Yes, Sir," stated Muncy and ended the call.

A brief time later, Muncy answered the doorbell, but no one was there, so she closed the door, thinking it was a prankster. But before she had taken a step, the doorbell rang again. Muncy opened the door, and a little voice shouted, "Hey lady, down here,"

Muncy looked down at a thirty-three-inch-tall figure clad in pale yellow shorts and a white blouse and thought that it was a little girl selling cookies, and said, "Thanks, but I have all the cookies I need,"

The girl stated, "My name is Darlene, and I'm not a kid; I just turned 34 yesterday, and your boss hired me to be your assistant."

Muncy called her boss and said, "Sir, you sent me an Ankle Biter for an assistant. I mean, she has to be three feet tall, if that,"

"Darlene has all the qualifications, so you're stuck with her,"

"Yes Sir," stated Muncy, and ended the call.

Muncy stood in her living room with its deep shag and ultramodern furniture, stared at Darlene, then said, "I'm gonna be in the backyard working on an article that will be published in the newspaper. I want you to bring me a pot of Hazelnut coffee and two raisin bagels with cream cheese, and I want to use the red napkins,"

In Muncy's back yard with its twelve foot high stockade fence she sat at the picnic table that had a red shade umbrella and smiled devilishly, thinking, "*With the coffee and things on the top shelf, there is no way that Ankle Biter will be able fulfill my order,*"

As Muncy was working on her article about the Andromeda Galaxy, she looked up, and there on the table was a red paper plate with four bagels with cream cheese, red napkins, two cups, and a chrome pot of coffee with Darlene sitting across from her.

Muncy then said, "I need you to check the mail, *thinking Ankle Biter would never be able to do that because the mailbox was way too high for her to reach. That's when I'll fire her scrawny hide,"*

Some three minutes later, Darlene handed Muncy the mail and asked, "Is it alright if I have my coffee and bagel now,"

"Sure, go ahead,"

As the sun was swiftly reaching the horizon, Muncy stared at Darlene, busy weeding the flower garden lining the perimeter of the backyard. Sat on the grass next to her and questioned, "How do you do it? I gave you every task someone your height would be impossible to do. But you did it faster than I could ever do,"

"Sheer determination to go forward," stated Darlene.

A tall, husky man in his early thirties, with shoulder-length brown hair clad in jeans and a white t-shirt, strolled in the backyard, and asked, "Hey Muncy, whose story have you put your name to this time,"

Greg LaMore," moaned Muncy, "I thought I told you to stay out of my yard,"

"You know you can't get rid of me," stated Greg, then let go a scream, looked down, and there was Darlene sinking her teeth into his ankle and hollered, "What did you do that for,"

Darlene said with a smile, "I'm an Ankle Biter; you want me to nibble on your other one."

"No, I don't," said Greg and quickly left.

Muncy noticed Darlene's ring and asked, "Wherever did you get that beautiful silver ring with all those diamonds,"

Darlene said, "It's called a stardust ring, and my boyfriend gave it to me as a reminder of his love. Now if you will excuse me, I have to find a place to live before it gets too dark,"

"I have an apartment in my basement if you are interested,"

"You bet!" shouted an excited Darlene.

Late that night, Darlene finished unloading the dishwasher and hollered, "Muncy, "I'm calling it a night," then entered her basement apartment and locked the door. She made a call on her digital watch and reported, "Reken, I found Muncy living in Arizona and is doing good but doesn't suspect who I am. I did a complete scan of the planet, and no one will catch the infectious hallucination infecting her,"

Reken warned, "Remember, the people of Earth have never seen a Sprite, so please be careful,"

"Yes, Sir," stated Darlene and ended the call. She spoke into her ring and said, "Power down for 5 minutes,"

As soon as the ring was off, two transparent wings appeared on Darlene's back; then she flew around the room saying, "It's been days since I've had a chance to exercise my wing muscles,"

The next morning Darlene was up early, went to Greg, and pounded on his front door. When Greg opened the door, Darlene shouted, "Down here, you backward, Balladonian."

Greg quickly looked around, then ushered Darlene inside, then asked, "Who are you?"

"I'm Darlene Comstock; I work for the Institute, in charge of the underground Tram. You, Sir, are from the planet Belladonna that was once controlled by the Hummer Gene, and don't tell me you're not because your speech betrays you. But what I want to know is, why are you after my friend Muncy?"

Greg asked, "How can a squirt like you have information about Planets that don't exist."

"You know they exist because that picture you have on your wall is Crystal City on the planet Dicapl, and the person in the Dark gray suit is you,"

Greg asked, "Why are you so protective of Muncy? Does she have some secret document about the Planetary Alliance locked up in her brain,"

"She's just a farm girl from the planet Pylee and is confused, so stay away from her if you know what's good for you,"

Greg glared down at Darlene and stated, "A little thing like you is threatening me, but all I have to do is step on you as I would a bug,"

Darlene turned off her ring, flew up in Greg's face, and stated, "This little bug has a nasty stinger," she then said, "Ring, energy beam," Then landed several shots to Greg's chest and back."

When Greg picked up a pot to throw at Darlene, she thought, *"Whoa, time to leave," and flew out an open window,"* She landed on the front lawn, turned on her ring, and hollered, "You missed me," then dove to her right as another pot landed where she was standing. Darlene turned around, bent over, and said, "Hey Greg, I bet you five bucks you can't hit my sit-down,"

When Greg didn't throw a pot, she thought, "*I guess he ran out of cookware.*" But before she could straighten up, something hit her butt that sent her flying forward and did a face plant on the lawn. Darlene spit out the grass and looked up at a smiling Greg holding a cast iron pan. He then stated, "You can keep the fiver, but you are not going to stop me in my pursuit of Muncy,"

Darlene saw Muncy approaching Greg from behind with a frying pan in her hand. She hit him on the back of his head, which sent him stumbling forward. He turned around, holding his head, and asked, "What did you do that for,"

Muncy shook her pan at Greg and said, "Two can play this game. You even think of touching Darlene again, and next time, I'll use a baseball bat,"

When Greg returned to his house, Muncy turned to Darlene and asked, "Are you alright,"

"My pride is a little bruised, but I'll live; by the way, do you have a pillow that I can use to sit on during the morning meal?"

"That afternoon, Muncy took Darlene to downtown Wickenburg to treat her to an ice cream sundae to thank her for her dedication to her work. While Darlene was enjoying her frozen treat, she heard a familiar voice say, "You call this stuff ice cream? I don't. It's more like a chemical concoction that resembles ice cream and will most likely kill me,"

Darlene approached the booth and stared at a twenty-eight-inch-tall woman with short deep brown hair, clad in a strapless Paisley sun dress, giving the waitress a tough time. The petite woman saw Darlene squealed, sprang out of the booth, and gave her a hug saying, "What are you doing alive?"

Darlene said, "Kayli Aubrette, you're a sight for sore eyes; I was about to ask you what you are doing on Earth."

"I'm here because Reken received a message in his surveillance lab from an unknown source saying that you were dead, so he sent little ol me to check on Muncy,"

"As you can see, I'm very much alive, so grab your frozen chemical concoction and follow me,"

Back at her booth, Darlene stated, "Muncy, this is Kayli Aubrette, Kayli Aubrette, this is Muncy,"

Muncy asked, "Kayli, you are so adorable, how old are you? Five?"

Kayli grimaced, then stated, "Add twenty years to that if you please,"

A shocked Muncy stated, "You are twenty-five, that's impossible,"

Kayli climbed on the booth's seat where Muncy was sitting, knocked on her head, saying, "Hello, anybody home in there? I guess not,"

"Okay, I'm convinced about your age," stated Muncy.

Driving back to her home, Muncy asked, "Kayli, where are you from?"

Not wanting to tell Muncy where she was really from, Kayli stated, "Oh, here and there, but no particular place to stay just yet,"

Muncy suddenly slammed on her brakes to prevent hitting a horse that was in the middle of the road that had long, bone-white, shaggy hair and golden eyes with three-inch long fangs. Then stated, "That is the ugliest horse I have ever seen,"

Darlene stated, "That's no horse, so slowly back up."

"What do you mean it's not a horse? Of course, it is,"

"Horses have hoofs; that thing has massive paws, so step on the gas and get us out of here,"

Kayli stated, "We have to kill it before that Snow Wolf attacks the people of Earth," two wings suddenly appeared on Kayli's back as she jumped out of the car. Darlene spoke into her ring, "Full power," as she stood on the left side of the Snow Wolf, ready to kill it.

Kayli quickly flew back and forth in front of the Wolf as Darlene fired a three-minute blast of energy at the venomous beast, causing the Snow Wolf to explode.

Kayli sat on the pavement, leaned against the left front tire of the car, out of breath, saying, "You gotta remember to keep your energy ring fully charged because that beast almost got me,"

Darlene bent forward, fluttered her wings, then said, "Kayli and I are Sprites, and that thing we just killed was a deadly Snow Wolf,"

Kayli stated, "Does this mean we don't have to hide who we are now that your friend knows? Dar? Hey Dar, can the silent treatment and answer me,"

Kayli stood, walked to the other side of the car, and froze in horror when she saw the second Snow Wolf had Muncy and Darlene pinned to the side of the vehicle. She whispered, "Can you take off your ring and throw it to me so I can kill that beast?"

Afraid the snow wolf would attack if she moved, Darlene slowly shook her head no.

Suddenly, six shots rang out, and the beast fell to the pavement dead, three feet from Darlene and Muncy. A tall man in his early sixties carrying a three-O-Three rifle helped the women to their feet and asked, "Are you ladies alright,"

The stranger stared at Darlene's wings, knelt in front of her, and asked, "Are you a real Pixie,"

Concerned that the man would capture and lock her up, she hesitated for a minute before nodding yes.

The man smiled and asked, "Would you mind if I touched your wings?"

"Sure, but we should burn that Snow Wolf before someone else sees it,"

Kayli stated, "Hey, you guys alright? Did it get any of its saliva on you?"

The man stated, "Whoa, you have a Pixie friend, far out,"

Once the Snow Wolf was destroyed and the stranger had left. Muncy gazed at the two Sprites and said, "I know you two. Kayli, you're from the planet Pylee and are on the Institute Security. Darlene, you run the Institute underground Tram, but I should know who Steve T Rogers is, but I don't right now,"

Darlene stated, "That was a close call. Now let's go home,"

2

JoJo to the rescue

At home, Muncy went into the backyard to write more in article. She took a swallow of her green iced tea, and a wave of dizziness swept over her for ten seconds and saw a rugged-looking man six feet tall, with deep brown curly hair, standing in front of her, trying to warn her about something. But she couldn't understand what he was saying. When she came, too, she was lying in the grass with Greg on top of her. But before she could scream for help, Darlene and Kayli were shouting, "Get off her," and hitting him with sticks they found in the yard.

Greg rolled off Muncy, slowly rose to his feet, and kicked Kayli in her side, sending her flying several feet before she hit the ground, screaming in pain.

Darlene accessed her energy ring and hit Greg with a mild energy charge saying, "Back off before I turn you into ashes,"

"Big talk for a runt," stated Greg, "But I'll do what I want, and you can't stop me, Shrimp," then approached a groggy Muncy.

Darlene let go another blast of energy from her ring, singing Greg's left shoulder, then stated firmly, "You make another stupid move, and you are history. One more thing, turn off your interstellar jammer before I level that poor excuse you call home."

Just then, a tall, well-dressed man in his late twenties with short brown hair, with a slight British accent approached Greg saying, "I see you're brave when harassing women, but how are you with a Nurd,"

Greg smiled, then said, "Nurds are my specialty," then approached him.

The Nurd took an eight-inch-long black rod from his side pocket and rammed it into Greg's side, sending a charge of electricity through his body. Then asked, "Had enough,"

Greg went to take a swing at the Nurd; he ducked and sent another charge of electricity through Greg's body that knocked him to the ground in agonizing pain.

A grateful Muncy gave the Nurd a hug, saying, "Reken, how did you manage to get through Greg's jammer,"

Reken smiled, saying, "Nurds rule while everyone else drools. Society won't admit it, but without nerds, we would still be using stone knives and hammers. Because we are the ones who invented motorcars, electric lights, and space travel. In other words, Greg is no match for me; hey, I gotta go,"

Muncy helped Kayli to her feet, checked her for broken bones than had her take a hot shower to ease the soreness. Darlene and Kayli then went for an ice cream sundae, and Muncy stepped in the shower and let the hot water run down her back to ease her stress.

Then her pink robe was thrown over the frosted shower door, and Greg said, "Put this on and meet me in the living room,"

A soaking wet Muncy entered her living room, which had pine furniture with deep blue pillows clad in her robe, shouting, "How dear you barge in my home and practically drag me out of the shower,"

Greg said in a strong tone, "Shut up and listen to me. You see this eight-inch-long black rod I have in my hand. It's called a Stem Rod and can inflict great pain. However, it has a companion called a Neuro Patch that will enhance the intense pain in a person's body. So, you are going to do what I say, or you will wish you had,"

Muncy pointed to the door, saying, "Get out of my house, you piece of twisted human garbage,"

Greg pointed the rod at Muncy, saying, "Allow me to demonstrate,"

Muncy fell to the floor, shrieking in anguish for twenty seconds. Greg then stated, "You see, I wasn't going to kiss you when you were lying on the grass, I put a Neuro Patch on your back, oh and it won't come off easily,"

"I suppose you are going to use it to force me to satisfy your fleshly desires."

"Nothing as carnal as that; I want you to hack into the Institute's computer and release some prisoners,"

"How am I gonna do something like that when I don't even know what the Institute is,"

"Don't play dumb with me, Muncy, because you know exactly what I am talking about. Oh, that pain you felt was the mild setting; this is high,"

Searing pain instantly coursed through Muncy's body, causing her to pass out.

Muncy came too ten minutes later, looked at Greg, and said, "If I could hack into the Institute's mainframe computer, I would, but I'm on the other side of the galaxy, and they don't make a computer powerful enough to reach 2.5 million light years, and a portal, a two-dimensional gateway will distort the signal. So, you can shoot me with pain until the sun goes nova. Oh, just FYI, The Galaxy Sentinel will roast your hide when he finds out what you are doing to one of his staff."

Muncy realized her robe had opened when Greg shot her with the stun rod, closed it, saying, "Creep," and felt a mini stun gun in her pocket, then said, "You can zap me with that thing-a-ma-bob all you want, but I will not stoop to your level. However, if you will do something for me, I just might be able to hack into the Institute's mainframe without being forced,"

"In other words, one hand washes the other," stated Greg, "So, what do you want me to do?"

Muncy sat on the couch, allowed most of her left leg to show, patted the deep blue cushion next to her, saying, "Sit,"

When Greg sat beside her on the couch, Muncy placed her bare leg on Greg's, held his hands, saying, "Why don't we get to know each other better? I'll go in the bedroom and get ready then you come in when I say okay,"

In Muncy's bedroom she took her robot and crawled in her canopy bed, then said, "OK, I'm ready,"

As soon as Greg walked into the bedroom, Muncy shot him with the stun gun, sending him to the floor out cold. She put her robe on then made a phone call and said, "Hey, Joanna Josephine Joplin, I need your help at my place right away,"

"It's JoJo, and what kind of trouble did you get into this time,"

"Just get here as fast as you can,"

A nicely built woman, of medium height, with short brown hair, in her early twenties. Dressed in loose-fitting jeans and a long sleeve white blouse entered the bedroom ten minutes later. Saw Greg on the floor, bound and gagged, and Muncy in her robe. Then questioned, "I know what it looks like, but you better start from the beginning."

Muncy handed JoJo the Stem Rod and said, "This Jerk was using this to force me into doing something underhanded. So, I tricked him, stunned him, and tied him up. But what I want you to do is get this Neuro patch off my back,"

JoJo stated, "Is that all you wanted me to do," took hold of the patch and ripped it off.

Muncy screamed, "Take it easy on the skin, will ya!"

JoJo showed Muncy the red 2-inch-long patch and stated, "You're fortunate the glue on this patch had seen better days. Why don't you brew some coffee while I free Gruesome."

JoJo untied Greg and said, "When you treated me to a fabulous dinner on the planet, Belladonna, I had no idea you were going to harass Muncy when you asked me to help you get to Earth."

Greg snapped back, "What I do on this planet is my business, not yours,"

"It is my business because I helped you get here, now back off from bugging Muncy before you have Thor, the Galaxy Sentinel, after you,"

Greg smiled sinisterly and said, "That wimp, of a Galaxy Sentinel, doesn't know what's going on this far away from the Planetary Alliance. But if you breathe a word to Thor, I'll let it be known that you work the red-light district in Aargau City on the Planet Pomona, which will destroy your credibility. Then while you are busy trying to straighten out that, I'll spread around how you claimed you traveled back in time to 1920. Which means they'll put you on the funny farm for the rest of your life,"

"Tell me why you are after Muncy when all she does is run the underground Tram at the Institute,"

Greg walked away without saying a word.

In the living room, JoJo took a swallow of her coffee, then inquired, "Muncy, your boss, Rose, is wondering when you are going to report back to work."

A puzzled Muncy took a swallow of her coffee and then said, "I don't work for Rose," Muncy dropped her flowered coffee cup and held her head as a wave of dizziness swept over her. She saw the same man warning her about something, but she couldn't figure out what he was saying.

Muncy opened her eyes, looked at JoJo, and said, "I never told anybody, but my brain is a bit scrambled to where I have difficulty remembering my past, and I hallucinate."

"What did you see when you were hallucinating?"

"I saw a man trying to warn me about something, but his words were garbled."

"What is your relationship with Greg? Are you bed buddies, and is the Stem Rod a kinky way of having fun with a guy?"

"That guy is barf city," stated Muncy, "And I have no idea why he is attracted to me outside the fact that he wants me to hack into The Institute's mainframe and release a few prisoners,"

JoJo asked, "Were you ever in the caves of Planet PX-12 in the Blue Ringed System here of lately? Because there is an infectious blue fungus in that cave that's causing people to have Memory loss and hallucinate."

"I'm not sure,"

"OK, let's start from the beginning. Rose took you to the Planet Dicapl to pick up supplies for the underground tram. You gave the supplies to Rose and told her that you needed some time off and vanished. My question is, who did you meet in the Dicapl Hardware?"

Muncy thought momentarily, then said, "A man who was too free with his hands asked me if I could fly him to PX-12 because he wasn't feeling too good. I told Rose that I needed some time off so I could pilot his craft to Planet PX-12. However, I wound up taking him to a rocky area of the planet instead of the city, as he said when I met him. When I landed, I felt a prick on my right arm and passed out. From then on, things are sketchy. I don't think he did anything to me while I was passed out. But I think it has something to do with the Institute, Greg, and that guy somehow."

JoJo stated, "If you weren't in those caves, then the guy you picked up was, and he transferred the infection to you. He most likely injected you with a sedative, so you wouldn't see which way he went after he dumped you out of his star car. Wait a minute; the guy injected you with a drug so you wouldn't remember that he was going to use you as a drug courier. The meeting place was most likely the caves of PX-12. You realized what was going on and hid the drugs. Greg wanted you to hack into the Institute's mainframe so that you would be caught. Then someone at the Institute would drag you into one of the underground caves and do whatever it took to get you to tell him where you hid the drugs. But first, you have to get rid of that infection. Do you have a bathtub?"

"I have a shower stall that I can lie down in,"

"That will have to do. Take everything off and lie down in the shower."

Some five minutes later, JoJo entered the bathroom carrying ten gallons of a deep blue gelatinous goo and covered Muncy with it, saying, "This is Doc Chrissy's remedy for infection."

Muncy asked, "How long do I have to be in this sStevely gunk,"

"For about an hour, oh, don't worry if it heats up, that just means it is working,"

The warmth from the goo put Muncy to sleep, but she woke with a start when Kayli entered the bathroom, saw her engulfed in a gob of something, and ran out screaming, "A monster is eating Muncy; run for your lives before it gets you!"

JoJo caught Kayli and explained, "A monster is not eating Muncy; she is being treated for an infection."

Kayli grumbled. "Way to go, JoJo; at least you could have done was warn us Sprites; now I have to change my undies. Thanks a lot."

JoJo casually entered the bathroom, knocked on the hard shell that once was a soft goo, and said, "For some unexplainable reason, the soft gelatinous goo has turned hard. I can get some of my male buddies here to break you out of it."

Muncy stated, "Don't you dare bring a man in here when I am indecent."

JoJo stated, "The longer it sits, the harder it will get."

Muncy screamed, "Joanna Josephine Joplin, you get me out of this stuff, or I'll tell everyone that you sleep with the light on because you're afraid of the dark,"

"That's past tenth, and I see the infection in your body is gone. All you have to do is stand, and the shell will easily crack,"

Muncy stood saying, "You were testing me to see how I would react around men when I'm in my birthday suit. Well, how did I do? Yes, I hid the drugs in the cave on PX-12, and yes, that guy grabbed my posterior and then said it was an accident."

JoJo asked, "I know you, Muncy. You didn't just pass it off as no big deal and retaliate some way."

"OK, it was more than a little tweak, so I cold cocked him, then hid the drugs."

JoJo stated, "."

"And I hid the guy's pants and shirt. No man gets fresh with me and gets away with it."

JoJo asked Kayli, "Where is Sprite, Darlene?"

"Darlene said she would grab some sun in the backyard when we returned from Chaparral Homemade Ice Cream and Café."

"She's not in the backyard nor the house," stated Muncy.

Muncy marched to Greg's home, pounded on the front door, and screamed, "Open this door, you poor excuse of a human!"

Greg opened the door clad in a pair of jean cut-offs, munching on a ham sandwich, and asked, "You bellowed oh boisterous one?"

"What did you do with Darlene?"

"You mean that pesty friend of yours? Don't know, don't care," stated Greg.

Muncy spotted Darlene's energy ring on Greg's mahogany coffee table, pushed her way past Greg, picked it up then demanded, "If you don't know where she is. What is her ring doing on your coffee table?"

"Oh yeah, that's right, I had one of my friends drop that Sprite thing of yours ten miles north of Everett Rodo Area,"

"You what?" shouted Muncy, "There's nothing out there but Mountain lions, scorpions, and tarantulas," then ran out the door to fetch JoJo and Kayli.

3

Trouble with Greg

Muncy returned home and reported, "JoJo, Greg told me he had one of his friends leave Darlene in the desert north of the Chaparral Rodeo, and we have to go find her."

"Darlene is a Sprite and will fly back, so there's no big deal," stated Kayli.

JoJo stated, "Something is wrong because Darlene is a fast flyer and should have been back by now. We need to get two four-wheelers and search for her. Kayli, we'll need you to do an Ariel search once we're out there."

In a scorching one hundred and twenty degrees, JoJo had a yellow four-wheeler, and Muncy had a red one. They parked beside each other, and JoJo stated, "Kayli, take some water with you and fly in a circle and let us know what you see. Muncy and I will drive around in hopes of spotting her."

Some forty-five minutes later, Kayli landed on the back of Muncy's vehicle and reported, "I saw something about a mile east of here."

But it was a rock with some brush to resemble a Sprite. JoJo radioed Muncy saying, "I spotted vultures circling west of my position."

Some twenty- minutes later, Muncy slammed on the breaks, jumped out, and ran to Darlene's crumpled body under a bush. She then shouted, "Kayli, get me the water from my cart!"

JoJo rushed to Muncy, knelt, and asked, "How is she doing?"

"She's alive, contact Moon Base 23 and ask Calistus to open a portal so we can get Darlene some medical attention,"

"I can't because of interference."

Kayli inquired, "Why didn't she fly home? I know that's what I would have done."

JoJo touched Darlene's wings, saying, "I don't think she can fly."

"Don't be silly; of course, Darlene can fly. That's what her wings are for," stated Kayli.

JoJo stated, "Darlene's wings are too limp, meaning Greg did something to them before he dumped her way out here."

Muncy held Sprite Darlene in her arms and asked, "Kayli, I know you are a little bit of a thing, but can you drive the four-wheeler if I rig the gas and break,"

"You bet,"

Back in Muncy's home, she lay Sprite Darlene on her bed, put her nightclothes on her, and gave her a drink of water.

Sprite Kayli sat on the bed to comfort her friend and stated, "We Sprites are frail because our Physiology isn't like a human and can't handle a lot of pressure. That's why we invent games like Tree Dodging, Belly Skimming, and Boulder Racing."

A puzzled Muncy questioned, "Please explain to me how you race a rock,"

Kayli stated, "We find a long steep hill, place a four-foot-tall boulder at the top. A Sprite stands five feet in front of it and runs down the hill with the boulder chasing him. The Sprite that gets to the bottom fasted without being smushed by winds. Sprite Marry Bell Bright holds the record for Boulder Racing. But she hasn't mastered Tree Dodging; I mean that Sprite has smacked into more trees than you can count."

Muncy stated, "I'm gonna hate myself in the morning for asking this, but what in the world is Tree Dodging,"

Kalie giggled, saying, "A bunch of us Sprites gather at the edge of a forest. A course through the trees is marked out, and the Sprite who can fly through the trees the fastest without smacking into something winds.'

Muncy stated, "I don't even want to know what Belly Skimming is."

Two days later, Kayli disguised herself as a small boy and followed

Greg when he left his house that evening. At 101 West Mohave Street, Greg entered a park, sat by a bush, and vanished.

Kayli took a mini scanner from her purse and scanned the area for signs of portal residue. She then hid in a large bush and waited until Greg returned.

Some two hours after Greg left, a deluge of rain fell for an hour; Kayli looked up and said, "I know I am to give thanks in all things, so Lord, thank you for the bath,"

Around three in the morning, a bright flash of light emanated from the same spot Greg disappeared. When the light faded, Greg was standing there with a clear plastic bag filled with small white packets. Kayli muttered, "He's selling drugs on Earth. But there is no logical reason in that."

Kayli took flight and dive-bombed Greg with rocks and sticks, trying to get him to drop the plastic pouch. When he did, Kayli snuck a packet out of the pouch and scurried away.

Around five that morning, Kayli walked in the back door all smiles. JoJo almost choked on her coffee when she saw Kayli and asked, "What in the world have you been up to besides getting into trouble."

Kayli held up a white packet and said, "I followed Greg last night, and he was transported somewhere, and when he returned, he had a plastic bag stuffed with these. But what I can't figure out is why Greg is selling Drugs this side of the galaxy."

JoJo stated, "With Greg running his interstellar jammer twenty-four-seven, I'd say he's a drug relay. But why is he after Muncy,"

"He's not after her; he's just a pain in her sit-down," stated Kayli.

Muncy entered the kitchen clad in her powder blue babydoll PJs, poured herself a mug of coffee, took a swallow then said, "The Planetary Alliance can track someone with drugs without problems. But when the drugs are sent to someplace like Earth through a teleporter and are hidden in an interstellar jammer's magnetic field, they lose track. Then all the drug carrier has to do is find some dummy to deliver the goods to the buyer." Muncy glanced at Kayli and asked, "You look like you played deluge in that downpour last night."

"I tracked Greg to his teleporter point last night and discovered he's a druggy, and here's the proof,"

Muncy stared at the packet of drugs as she held it up and stated, "There has to be a logical reason because I do not believe Greg is stupid enough to do this."

Muncy stared at the mist coming out of the computer outlet on the wall and asked, "What in heaven's name is wrong with that computer jack? JoJo, get the fire extinguisher,"

In seconds, the mist formed into a human shape, then coalesced into a woman six feet tall with long brown wavy hair, clad in a long forest green dress. She smiled and shook Muncy's hand, saying, "Thor sent me. I'M Dina, a self-sustaining three-dimensional computer program. I can upload myself into any computer or through a computer jack or be a solid woman, as you can see."

Kayli squealed, "Dina! How have you been?"

Dina quickly shrunk to Kayli's size and gave her a hug saying, "Doing good. Mary Bell finally won the Tree Dodging tournament,"

A shocked Kayli stated, "You're kidding? Mary Bell won Tree Dodging? Well, what do you know, miracles do exist."

JoJo asked, "Why did the Galaxy Sentinel send you instead of a real human? No offense,"

Dina returned to her normal size and stated, "None taken, if Thor sent a real human, the boss of the underworld would have known and informed the dealers to shut down. By sending me, they won't have a clue what's going on."

Muncy asked, "How in the world did you travel 2.5 million light years in such a short time,"

"Thor opened a portal to one of Earth's communications satellites; I stepped through it, entered Earth's satellite system, then had fun navigating the vast Internet connections."

Muncy stated, "So Thor is aware of what's happening on this side of the galaxy,"

"More than you know. Hey, after traveling 465,000,000,000 miles, I am starved,"

Muncy stated, "But you're a computer-generated avatar, and they don't eat food,"

"I have the ability to turn a chicken breast into pure energy, so make with the grub,"

Muncy handed Dina a pan of lasagna; she sat at the kitchen counter and ate the whole pan."

An upset Muncy stated, "Hey, I expected you to save some of that for dinner tonight,"

Dina stated, "Now that I am fully charged, I'll upload into Greg's computer to see what he's up to. Oh, thank you for the food, and just to let you know, I normally don't eat human food, but this was an emergency,"

With Dina in Greg's computer, Muncy stated, "I better get dressed and make the morning meal."

After the morning meal, Darlene finished her tea, then marched to Greg's house and pounded on the front door, saying, "Open up, you poor excuse of a human,"

Greg opened the door, looked down at Darlene, and said, "Oh good, you made it back alive."

Darlene flew up and got in Greg's face saying, "I know what you are up to, and I'm here to tell you that it won't work. Oh, do you wanna stand still for a moment? I want to give you Something,"

Darlene flew across the street, then flew towards Greg as fast as she could, hitting him between his pockets and sending him down on his knees in great pain."

When Greg turned around, there was a tall willowy woman dressed in loose-fitting black slacks and a white blouse smiling at him and handing him a pack of ice, saying, "Sprites can be pesty at times. Here's an ice pack for your injury."

"What are you doing in my home, woman?"

"I walked in while you were talking to Darlene. I'm Dina, and I'm here to service your computer. That's if it is alright with you,"

"My computer is working just fine; what I need is food."

"Food it is," stated Dina and cooked the morning meal for Greg fit for a king. Then after he ate, she took off his shirt, and massaged his shoulders and asked, "Why do you have Muncy *Bilmore* as a Courier on your computer when you give her all kinds of trouble? Shouldn't you be treating your faithful worker with respect? Oh, those sexy pictures you have on your computer of Muncy sunbathing in her Backyard, I deleted them. Now you can take cute pictures of me,"

A shocked Greg asked, "How did you get by the password on my computer?"

"You have a password on that archaic thing you call a computer?"

Greg stated, "Woman, I don't have nasty photos of Muncy on my computer, and I don't want one of you; thanks for the morning meal, but I think you should go."

Dina stood behind Greg, placed her hand on his back, reached inside his body, and was about to stop his heart. She decided not to, thinking, "*I better not just yet,*" She gave him a kiss and said, "Oh, I live with Muncy."

A few minutes later, Dina sat at the picnic table in Muncy's Backyard, stared at her, and said, "Girl, we need to talk."

Muncy stopped writing her article, looked at Dina, and said, "I'm all ears,"

Dina inquired, "Why are you delivering drugs for Greg and you have got to stop letting Greg take pictures of you when you have barely anything on,"

An indignant Muncy stated, "I do not deliver drugs for that creep, and I definitely don't pose for him at all. However, I do put on something tiny and lay in the sun, besides, who's going to see me with a twelve-foot high stockade fence around my Backyard,"

"News flash, Muncy, I just came from inside Greg's computer, and he had two dozen pictures of you in your skimpy attire and has you logged in as his drug Courier. Don't worry, I deleted those pictures."

Muncy felt a wave of dizziness sweep over her and passed out. She woke an hour and twenty-two minutes later, lying face down in the Backyard. Dina helped her in the house, gave her a cup of hot tea then asked, "Do you remember what happened?"

"All I remember is being faint, passing out, and coming too just a few minutes ago."

"While we were talking, you were teleported someplace, most likely to deliver the drugs Greg picked up a day or two ago."

"I did not have any of Greg's drugs," affirmed Muncy.

"Oh, but you did, just before you slowly faded, an eight-and-a-half by eleven manila folder appeared in your left hand,"

Muncy stated, "If that's so, let's take Greg out now because I hate being used,"

Dina held Muncy's right arm, saying, "Hold on Feisty Pants. If we take out Greg now, the top man will escape. So, let's deal with him taking pictures of you first."

Muncy lay on her stomach in her usual skimpy attire while Dina morphed into a small bird, scanned the area, and found a tiny camera sticking out of a fence post. Muncy ran to the post, smashed the camera, dressed in jeans and a green t-shirt, and pounded on Greg's front door.

When he opened it, Muncy shoved the demolished camera in his face saying, "How dare you take pictures of me sunbathing,"

Greg slammed his fist in Munchy's stomach, then hauled her inside and slammed the door, saying, "Get rid of that woman Dina, or you will be among the missing,"

Muncy stated, "You don't tell me what to do, Mister."

Greg landed a hard right cross to Muncy's face, then threw her across the living room, landing on the coffee table. Muncy staggered to her feet, battling the pain. But before she could do anything, Greg hammered Muncy's body with roundhouse kicks until she lay motionless on his brown living room rug. Greg then said, "You don't come to my door and threaten me." He then threw her body over the stockade fence.

JoJo had returned with the Sprites, saw Muncy lying on the ground, and ran to her aid. She called Dina to help her bring Muncy into the house, then stormed into Greg's home.

Greg asked, "You want what I just gave Muncy? If not, get out of my house woman,"

JoJo called 911 and said, "The man at this address needs serious medical attention. Ended the call, took the broad sword from over the fireplace, and sliced Greg's arms, legs, and back. Then said, "You come near Muncy again, and you're a dead man."

In Muncy's home, JoJo threw the bloody sword on the kitchen counter, saying, "I just hacked up Greg for what he did to Muncy and threatening me. Don't worry he's still alive. By the way, how's she doing,"

"Dina stated, "She's alive but badly bruised,"

4

On the run

The next day Muncy walked into the kitchen in her yellow babydoll PJs, moaning, "I hurt in places where I didn't think I could hurt. JoJo, could you fix my morning meal for me? I'm gonna sit in the backyard and soak up the sun, and I don't care how many pictures Greg takes of me. Oh, by the way, where is Dina?"

JoJo stated, "She uploaded herself into the internet early this morning around five, and I haven't seen her since."

After Muncy finished her meal, she felt a gentle touch on her right leg. They glanced down and exclaimed, "Gideon Bear! What are you doing here?" Then picked up a two-foot-tall dark blue bear with round black eyes, a black nose, and a slit for a mouth. Dressed in a bright red kimono and Muncy gave him a squeeze.

Dina sat on Muncy's left and said, "I went back to the Institute and told Thor what was going on, so he sent Gideon the Avenging Bear to help,"

Just then, two men clad in black suits casually strolled in the backyard and up to Muncy. Dina whispered, "I'll go for help." and rushed off.

Muncy smiled politely and said, "I'm sorry I'm in my PJs, but what can I do for you, gents?"

One man stated, "You were told to get rid of the women in your home. Now do it," then slapped Muncy across the face.

Muncy rubbed the left side of her face saying, "If you two know what's good for you. Leave now before my protector, the Ninja Master, makes short work of you."

The man laughed and said, "All I see is a dumb-looking bear,"

Gideon flipped backward, landed on the picnic table with his katanas in his paws, and growled.

The man said with a smirk, "How cute, a holographic bear is going to slice me up,"

Gideon jumped on the man's right shoulder, sliced off his ear, did a back flip to the ground, and sliced the left leg of the other man. Jumped on Muncy's lap with his katanas pointing at the men.

Muncy stated, "My bear is not a hologram but my protector, you come around here again, and they'll need a magnifying glass to find the pieces."

After Greg's two thugs left, JoJo entered the backyard, clapping and saying, "Now that's what I call kicking butt. Way to go, Gideon!"

A short time later, a well dress man, five foot six feet tall, approached Muncy and asked her to stand. He then gave her a long kiss and hug.

Muncy pushed him away, saying, "Gideon, attack," but when the bear didn't move, she muttered, "Stupid bear," and slapped his face saying, "You do that again, you'll be spitting out your teeth,"

He smiled, saying, "I always loved seeing you in yellow."

Muncy then stated, "Hey, you're the man I see when I'm hallucinating."

"I'm your main squeeze Steve, or Sir Rogers, to everyone else,"

"You have me at a disadvantage because my memory isn't up to par right now,"

"I'm surprised you have a memory at all after what you've been through,"

Muncy stated slowly, "I know you,"

Steve sat on Muncy's right on the picnic table, gently placed his hand on her thigh, then said, "Take all the time you need to remember who I am. Does a jelly doughnut at Thuma's diner mean anything to you,"

"No, should it, but for some reason, I don't mind you touching my leg,"

Steve had Muncy turn so her back faced him; he massaged her shoulders until she lay back in his arms.

Some ten minutes later, Muncy stated, "You better stop doing that because it's giving me ideas,"

Steve stood saying, "Better luck next time, I guess, same time, same place tomorrow,"

Just as Steve's hand was on the gate, Muncy sprang to her feet shouting, "Steve, my main squeeze!" she ran, jumped, and landed with her legs straddling his waist and her arms around his neck, kissing him.

Steve tumbled to the ground with Muncy on top of him and asked, "You wanna get off me before someone sees us,"

Muncy stated, "Ask me if I care,"

A short time later, Steve and Muncy stood; she fixed her PJ bottoms and brushed the dirt off Steve as JoJo approached and questioned, "You two finished with your fleshly actions,"

Muncy said, "Hey, give me a break, will ya? I haven't seen him and a coons age,"

"You're a Christian and should not be involved in that kind of stuff with Steve before marriage."

"What's wrong with kissing my fiancé?"

"Do you want me to spell it out for you? Steve was in the process of taking off your PJ's and don't say he wasn't because I saw what was going on between you two. So, if you want to keep your job as head of the underground Tram, back off with the flesh with Steve."

"Steve said to JoJo, "I took a risk coming here under the guise of a space traveler to tell you guys that you stirred up a hornet's nest when you hacked up Greg. You've got two hours to pack my star car and head for the hills, or you're dead."

Dina approached Steve and asked, "What do you base your information on? I've been all over Earth's internet and the Alliance, and I haven't run across anything about the crime bass ready to strike revenge on Muncy and the others."

Suddenly something was tossed over the fence, Dina shouted, "Grenade!" and jumped on top of it as the others dove for cover, and there was a muffled poof."

Dina stood, stared at the grenade fragments sticking out of her stomach, and said, "Is everyone alright? It looks like I need my energy field updated. Steve, would you mind if I use the network connection in your star car to update myself,"

"Sure, go ahead,"

A spunky Darlene picked up a club and held it like a bat saying, "Let's show those thugs they can't push us around,"

Steve smiled and said, "Greg has three dozen men who are experts in inflicting pain to someone's body."

"Let them come because I laugh at pain."

Steve knelt, looked a Sprite Darlene in her eyes, and said, "With a little thing such as yourself. Your wings would be pulled off so you couldn't get away then you would be given to their two Rottweilers for a chew toy. Which means one dog would chomp on your shoulder, the other dog would most likely take your leg in his mouth, and the two would pull you apart."

Darlene put her club down, saying, "Can we go now,"

Steve asked, "You change your mind,"

"Yeah, you had me with my wings being pulled off; ouch!"

JoJo took Steve aside and said, "You don't love Muncy and you don't plain to merry her because all you are interested in is sex."

"How can you say those lies about me,"

"My friend Patty is an unwed mother because of your so called love. Oh, I have the names of the other women you so called loved. So back off,"

Steve shouted, "Everyone pack because we leave in 20 minutes!"

Later, Steve drove his red Tessler west on the Arizona freeway and just passed the Wickenburg exit. A young man in a black Chevy SUV kept blocking him from getting in the fast lane.

Muncy stated, "Don't let him get your goat, Sweetheart, because you're on Earth and not Haskell Prime."

"I've been trying to change lanes for the past half hour, and this jerk won't let me and may be one of Greg's men,"

Steve tried to enter the fast lane again, and the man in the SUV cut him off.

He snapped, "That's it, his butt is mine." and ordered. "Computer, engage energy barrier to full." He turned his steering wheel to the left, slamming the SUV into the Jersey barrier, ripping off his front fender, and severely damaging the left side of the car. Steve quickly stopped, got out, and asked the young man, "Are you alright?"

The tall thin young gentleman screamed, "Look what you did to my car; I'm gonna Sue you for everything you've got, Mr., because you're gonna pay dearly."

Some 25 minutes later, the Highway Patrol officer approached the young man in the SUV and asked him what happened. The man pointed to Steve and screamed at how he forced him into the Jersey barrier.

Steve calmly replied, "Officer, I don't know what this man's been smoking, but I did not force him into the Jersey barrier. If I did, there would be damage on the left side of my car, and as you can see, there isn't even a scratch, so how could I have done it."

The Officer examined Steve's car, then the black SUV, and stated to Steve, "You can go, Sir. It's evident that he lost control of his car and is trying to put the blame on you."

As Steve got in his car, he heard the man scream, "You're letting him go? He slammed his car into mine; he's lying; I tell you, he's lying,"

Several miles down the road, Kayli asked, "Why did you lie to the police officer,"

"I temporarily forgot who I was in Christ and slipped into my flesh. But thank you for reminding me how wrong I was. However, one has to be careful not to reveal who we are and where we're from because if that happens, the people of that planet will use us as test subjects, and I don't have to explain to you what that means."

Kayli stated, "You mean they would strip me naked, put me on my stomach and stick a probe up my sit-down."

"Something like that."

Hours later, on US-5 to the Baja Peninsula, Steve looked in the rearview mirror and muttered, "Oh crap! Highway Patrol, I guess I've been going a little bit too fast for their liking." Steve then ordered, "Bring Fusion reactor online and engage star drive. Set inertia dampening field to the maximum, retract wheels, and set a course for 45 degrees upward."

In less than a second, the Tessler car transformed into an interstellar star car and was out of sight.

Steve hovered the start car 30,000 feet above the planet, smiled, and said, "You have to get up pretty early in the morning to outsmart someone from Haskell Prime. Muncy, I think this is an excellent place to have a midday meal. Darlene, what will you have?"

"Give me a foot-long meat lovers Hoagies and a cup of black coffee."

Kayli stated, "I don't like Hoagies so I'll have a meat lovers Hero,"

Some 25 minutes later, Muncy finished her tuna sandwich and Iced tea; Steve finished his supernova energy drink when the car's scanner picked up a fast-approaching aircraft. He checked it and said, "We've got four F-22 Raptors closing on us fast. Tilted the start car sideways to avoid a sidewinder missile, engaged the star drive, circled around, came up behind the fighters, and flew between the two of them. He smiled and waved at the pilot in one of the Jets, then was out of sight in a flash.

Sometime later, Steve landed the star car in the desert, Sprite Kayli jumped out and flew skyward, hollering, "Alive! Yes, I'm alive!"

Muncy shouted, "Kayli, you be careful because you never know what wacko earthling is watching,"

"Okay I will."

Muncy turned to Steve and questioned, "Do you want to explain to me again why we're in the middle of nowhere?"

"A man from Earth told me to meet him here because he had some important information concerning alien abductions. I figured it may help to recover some of the people who have gone missing while visiting Earth."

Just then, a rifle shot rang out; Kayli screamed as she plummeted to Earth and slid along the sand.

Muncy rushed up to Kayli, cradled her in her arms then bandaged her wound.

A man in his late sixties with white hair and a beard screeched to a halt in his four-Wheeler next to Kayli and said, "It's mine,"

Steve stood behind the gentleman, leveled his energy rifle at the man, and stated, "Slowly drop that thing you call a weapon and put your hands up, or I'll vaporize you where you stand."

The man turned around with his hands raised, stared at Steve's gun, and stated, "I take it you're not from around here."

Steve questions, "Are you the one who contacted me concerning missing aliens,"

"I sure am, and that thing on the ground over there is mine; I shot it fair and square,"

"That thing, as you call her, is a Sprite and not a thing."

Muncy stood with Kayli holding her left hand, and stated, "You used deception to draw us here so you could shoot Kayli and cash in on some money."

"I sure did. I heard about you people and how you were friends with Pixies, so I figure she's mine now so hand her over!"

Kayli approached the man and kicked him in his shins, saying, "You shot me in my sit-down and ruined my favorite shorts!"

Steve vaporized the man's four-wheeler, then stated, "You're coming with us; I know a professor at an Institute who wants to do a study on a human from Earth."

Kayli giggled and asked, "Are they gonna strip him naked and shove a probe up his sit-down?"

Muncy stared at Kayli and stated, "You and I are gonna have to talk."

5

Kayli steppes in

An hour later, Steve landed on the tarmac, on the right side of the Institute building on a hidden planetoid. Handed the man from the desert to Thor, the Galaxy Sentinel, and said, "He's to be delivered to Professor Gutenberg on planet PX5, and Muncy will brief you on what it's happening on Earth. I'll talk to you later because there's a bed waiting for me."

Kayli looked up at the five-story red brick building on her right and thought about the welcome home gathering in the cafeteria. She turned left and walked in the massive Arboretum to find a quiet spot.

After the welcome home party, Tippy, a six-foot tall female Will-o-the-wisp resembling a six-foot Pixie with transparent wings was dressed in a beige socks suit, approached Muncy and stated, "You and I have to talk about your actions with Steve,"

"Isn't Rose, Thor's wife, the one who is supposed to be talking to me about my relationship with a guy? After all, she is head of the women at the Institute."

The Galaxy cafe is situated in a housing complex, a short walk through the woods in the back of the Institute. The two women ordered coffee, and Tippy stated, "I'm being trained for the next Galaxy Sentinel, so I'll be handling all the women's complaints and not Rose."

Muncy gave her a report concerning the underground Tram and how well things were operating. Tippy stopped her mid-sentence and said, "I'm aware of the excellent job you are doing with the underground Tram. However, this is about your relationship with Steve."

Muncy stated in defense, "I can explain my actions with Steve when I met him in my backyard on Earth,"

"JoJo didn't say anything to me about that, but I Will talk to her now that you mention it. What I want to talk to you about is there have been numerous reports of Steve leaving your house early in the morning. Which means he spent the night with you. When you were hired by the Institute to run the underground Tram, you were told that promiscuity would not be tolerated, but yet here you are sleeping with a guy from off the planetoid."

Muncy stated in defense, "I am not sleeping with Steve, and I haven't slept with a man since I gave my life to Christ. But because of his bad leg, I have to help Steve in the shower."

"Then you are in the shower with him,"

"The details of how I helped Steve's shower aren't important,"

"Why is Steve leaving your home early in the morning,"

"I have no idea,"

"How long have you been dating Steve?"

"I met him three weeks before Rose took me for supplies, and we hit it off right from the beginning. As far as Steve sleeping with me or staying in my home overnight isn't true."

"It was Sprite Mimi Iris of security who spotted Steve leaving your home early in the morning,"

"As I said, I didn't have Steve do a stayover at any time, and why he was leaving my home at that hour of the morning, I do not know."

A short time later, Muncy opened the door to her home and stood motionless for over a minute when she saw the destruction. She then picked up the pieces of her favorite pixie statue, sat on the floor, and cried.

Sprite *Missy* Wells, a 34-inch sprite with light brown hair clad in worn-out jeans and a white t-shirt. She poked her head in the door munching on a peanut butter, sardine, Jelly, and pickle sandwich, and hollered, "What happened to your beautiful home?"

"Hi, Missy," moaned Muncy.

Missy then cried, "Oh no, what happened to your magnificent Pixie statue?"

"I don't know,"

Missy took a bite of her sandwich, then said, "Don't do anything; I'll go for help." And flew out the door.

Some twenty-one minutes later, a mob of women from the Institute walked in the door led by Rose. She shouted, "Okay, ladies, it's time to go to work!" Rose took the smashed statue from Muncy and gave it to one of the ladies, saying, "Give this to Cathy so she can fix it. Muncy, you're coming with me to the Galaxy café because it's been way too long since you had the Institute's Specialty Burger."

At the café, the waitress put a hamburger platter in front of Muncy that had two three-quarter pound beef burgers, ketchup, relish, cheese, lettuce, tomato, onions, Pickles, and bacon on a Kaiser roll and a mountain of curly French fries on the side.

Rose said, "I was talking to Tippy; what have you gotten yourself into?"

"I have no Idea. All I know is I found myself living on Earth, next door to Greg, who constantly harassed me and took pictures of me sunbathing in my you know what in my backyard. Oh, he was using me as his drug courier without me knowing it."

"Did you do or say anything to Greg that gave him ideas you were interested in him?"

"No, I didn't,"

"Then how was Greg able to photograph you in some thin, slinky thing?"

"He had a hidden camera on my stockade fence. Okay, things went like this. A man who was too free with his hands when he was around me asked to fly him to PX-12, so I told you I needed some time off and took him to Planet PX-12. But wound up taking him to a rocky area of the planet instead of the city, like he asked. When I landed, I felt a prick on my right arm and passed out. From then on, things are sketchy. I don't think he got fresh with me while I was unconscious, but I'm not sure. I came to my census sometime later carrying some drugs. I hid them in The Cave and then found myself on Earth, living next door to Greg. But I lost track of large segments of time while I lived there, and it stopped when Steve found me on Earth."

Rose stated, "The man most likely injected you with a micro-neurotransmitter that put you in a hypnotic state when activated. This means someone could tell you something, and you would obey without question. By you living next door to Greg he was able to trigger the neurotransmitter anytime he wanted you to deliver some drugs for him. This way, you wouldn't have any memory of what happened and couldn't snitch on him."

The next thing Muncy knew, she opened her eyes, lying on a stretcher in the Infirmary with nothing on but a Johnny-coat and Rose saying, "Come on, Muncy, wake up, snap out of it,"

Muncy asked, "What am I doing here, and where are my clothes?"

"You suddenly started acting weird and walked out of the diner. I had security stun you and brought you to the Infirmary, and Chrissy removed the micro neurotransmitter from your right arm. She then gave you a complete physical while you were unconscious, and as far as she could see, no man took advantage of you sexually while you were in a hypnotic state."

After Muncy was released from the Infirmary, she entered the cafeteria for a cup of coffee and sat in a booth in the far left corner. A man six feet tall, with dark brown hair and rugged looking, sat across from her in the booth and said, "My wife told me about how you were mixed up with drug smuggling against your will. But this may work out to our advantage because now we may have an inroad to the organization and will be able to shut it down. However, be careful who you talk to outside of the Institute,"

"Thor, Sir, thank you for sending Steve to fetch us from Earth,"

"I didn't send Stevel because he's not one of the Institute's staff, and it would have tipped off the Underworld boss,"

"Steve said that you sent him,"

"I can assure you I didn't,"

Early the next day, Muncy slowly looked around at the solid rock walls and ceiling, sat in the driver's seat of the underground Tram, and bellowed, "Next stop, Smile Lake, all aboard,"

Steve tapped her right shoulder, saying, "I see you're back in the groove of things. You wanna meet me for lunch,"

"Oh, while you are here, I need to ask you something. Before I left with Rose for supplies. You were spotted by Sprite security leaving my home early in the morning. Can you tell me what you were doing in my home while I was in bed asleep?"

"Trust me when I say I was not in your house early in the morning."

"Then why does Sprite Security put in a report that you were seen leaving my home in the morning."

"I was enjoying the water at the beach on Smile Lake one day when Sprite Mimi floated by on her back and accused me of grabbing her butt. I told her I didn't, but she's been out to get me ever since."

"If you are going to be on this tram you need to sit,"

At the underground tram station of Smile Lake, two dozen wet Sprites piled in, giggling, and laughing. Muncy shouted, "King Mex's Kingdom, next stop."

When the Tram reached Mix's kingdom, some Sprites got off, and some got on, and the Tram was packed full.

Muncy shouted, "Lake Mary Bell, last stop,"

At Lake Mary Bell, all the Sprites quickly left; Muncy pulled a lever on her left side, causing the Tram to spin 180 degrees. Then she said, "I have to wait twenty minutes before I return to the main terminal."

Steve knelt by Muncy, kissed her lips then said, "Twenty minutes is just enough time for us to make out."

Muncy pinched Steve's neck, saying, "You know what that will lead into, and I don't want to go down that road with you."

Steve sat in Muncy's lap, and put his arms around her, saying, "There is no one around, so relax and let's enjoy each other."

While Steve was forcing himself on Muncy, he was suddenly ripped out of her lap and thrown to the back of the Tram.

Steve slowly stood, stared at Tippy standing by Muncy, and said, "Well, well, well, if it isn't the insect trying to be a human."

Tippy stated, "Your security pass for this planetoid has been revoked.

"For what reason?" screamed Steve.

"Some discrepancies have been found in your Planetoid Access Application."

"Why all the red tape? I don't have to jump through hoops on other worlds,"

"This is a military-controlled Planetoid run by the Galaxy Sentinel, so clearance is necessary."

"Then tell the Galaxy Sentinel Steve Rogers wants to see him,"

Tippy smiled and stated, "You are looking at the Galaxy Sentinel,"

Steve's mouth suddenly dropped open, then whispered, "You are ah, him, ah her?"

Tippy seized Steve by his shirt collar, had security drag him away, and locked him up until a formal hearing could be heard. She then stared at Muncy and asked, "Are you alright?"

Muncy was putting her blouse back on as she said, "Yeah, and thanks,"

A puzzled Tippy stated, "You say you are a modest Christian, yet you allow Steve to handle the merchandise. Why?"

Muncy lowered her head, saying, 'It's what I have to do when he's kissing me, and I have no choice but to let him,"

"You do have a choice and how far did Steve get?"

"I'd rather not talk about it,"

"In other words, you were willing to go all the way with him whether you wanted to or not."

"I never got in bed with Steve and I never will; now, can we change the subject," stated Mancy.

"No, we can't. If you are having a problem with Steve, out with it."

"Steve is sweet, kind, always talks about his family and how great they are and goes overboard when he's helping me with a project. However, something inside of me wants to run from him as fast as I can,"

"I'd listen to that urge to run if I were you; now, if you will excuse me, I have things to do."

A man clad in black pants and neatly combed black hair boarded the Tram and sat two seats behind Muncy and remained quiet.

About Two hours later, at the main terminal, Kayli, dressed in her white, one-piece bathing suit, glanced at her watch, and wondered, *"Where is the Tram? Muncy is never this late."*

Kayli stared down the dark tram tunnel and thought, "I guess I have to fly in there to find out what happened to Muncy, and I pray I don't have to fly the entire 800 miles to Lake Mary Bell."

Somewhere around a mile and a half in the tram tunnel, Kayli found the stopped Tram, but no Muncy. She touched her computer watch and said, "Tippy, I found the underground tram but no Muncy."

"Tippy here, can you drive the Tram to Lake Mary Bell and pick up the Sprites? I'll alert Tom, chief of security, and have him organize a search party."

Kayli sat in the Tram's driver's seat and pulled the lever on the left to turn it around but spun it around twice. She held her head, saying, "Woah, which wasn't right. Let me try that again without making myself dizzy,"

With the Tram pointed back to the lake, Kayli pushed the throttle forward, catapulting the train forward at over nine hundred miles an hour. She then stood on the break closed her eyes, and prayed, "Please, Lord make it stop so they don't find my mangled little body in the wreck,"

With everyone on, Sprite Mimi, dressed in a modest two-piece Paisley bathing suit, questions, "Kayli, Why isn't Muncy driving? Is she sick?"

"She's missing, and I have to drive you guys back."

Mimi saw how nervous Kayli was, stood up, and hollered, "Listen up everybody, we have a problem, Muncy is missing, and Kayli has to drive the Tram back to the station. So, I want everybody to quiet down and pray that this isn't our final ride,"

The joyful chatter ceased as Mimi Set behind Muncy, placed her hand on her right shoulder, saying, "You can do it,"

Kayli whispered, "I'm scared because I've never done anything like this before. What if I mess up and wind up killing everybody,"

Mimi stated, "Take a deep breath, and remember the scripture that says I can do all things through Christ who strengthens me."

With the Tram pointing in the right direction, Kayli eased the throttle forward and arrived back at the main terminal two hours later instead of the normal thirty-five minutes.

Kayli shouted, "Institute Tram Station, everybody off! The tram will be down until further notice."

All the Sprites thanked Kayli and somberly exited the Tram. Mimi gave her a hug saying, "That's the first time in my life that I've seen that group of Sprites quiet."

"You mean I scared the crap out of them. You wanna help me clean this place up then we can go for coffee at the Galaxy Café."

6

A hurting Muncy

At the Galaxy Café, Kayli and Mini ordered Ice cream sodas and a plate of fried Potato Buds. Kayli popped a Potato bud in her mouth and asked, "Is it true that you saw Steve leaving Muncy's home early in the morning?"

"I shouldn't say this, but I have a lot of files on my computer watch about Steve. My boss, Moonbeam, told me to keep an eye on him, so I am logging about every step he takes. Here, I'll show you."

Mimi accessed her computer watch and projected on the café wall a five-by-eight-color aerial photo of Steve leaving Muncy's home. Then asked, "Do you believe me now? I have about seventy-five gigabytes of information stored on my computer watch concerning Stevel's actions around other Sprite women, holding meetings with various shady characters from off-world, and having been seeing Muncy Carlos secretly. But I've told you too much already."

Kayli questioned, "How is the search going concerning Muncy?"

"If she's on this planetoid, we'll find her."

"Could she have been kidnapped and dragged into the underground ruins of the ancient city Odessa,"

"That's where they started their search, but there's a lot of territory to cover."

Kayli stated, "I've got an idea where Muncy is, you wanna come with me?"

"I wish I could, but I have to report for work in twenty minutes."

A short time later, Kayli drove the Tram to where she found it, took a flashlight, looked for evidence of where Muncy was taken, and found a button on the left side of the Tram.

Some 20 minutes later, Kayli had a pocket full of buttons and objects that Muncy dropped and stared at a small group of ruins some three hundred yards in front of her and a light in one of the windows.

Kayli shut off her flashlight and crawled on her hands and knees to a window in an old, dilapidated stone building. When she peeked in the window, a bloodied Muncy was tied to a chair in the middle of the room, and a man was beating her with his fist and screaming, "Tell me where you hid It!"

Muncy cried, "Hid what? Tell me what I was supposed to hide."

The man smacked Muncy across the face saying, "Don't play dumb with me, lady. Now tell me!"

Kayli scanned the large cavern, made a commotion on the opposite side of the ruins, and waited for the men to investigate. When they did, Kayli flew into the building, untied Muncy, and used every ounce of strength she had to help her to escape.

Hunkered down under a pile of rubble some distance away, Kayli ripped the sleeves of her gray blouse off and cleaned up Muncy. She removed her backpack and opened a Styrofoam box full of potato buds, saying, "It's not much, but it'll help until I can get you out of here." Kayli then let Muncy use her backpack for a pillow and went to sleep.

An hour later, Sprite Kayli woke Muncy saying, "We gotta go."

After a short prayer for help. Muncy stood to her feet but struggled to walk because of all the beatings she took. Set on the ruins of a house and said, "You might as well leave me here because I can't make it."

Sprite Kayli stated, "We can do all things through Christ. You stand, I'll fly up to your shoulders, put my arms around you and help you walk."

"You're only twenty-eight inches tall and I'm five and a half feet, so how can you help me,"

"You either let me help you, or I'll die here trying to protect you. Now let's go,"

When they were one hundred feet from the Tram, shots from an energy pistol struck a nearby rock, and a man shouted, "There they are, don't let them get away!"

Kayli stated in Muncy's ear, "We're going to make it. Just don't look back,"

Once on the Tram, one of the men was about to board it when Kayli threw the throttle forward, throwing him off.

At the Tram station, under the housing complex, Kayli called for help. In seconds, the Tram was crowded with people overjoyed that Muncy was alive.

An exhausted Kayli stared at the crowd wanting to say, "Hey, what about me? I'm the one who saved her," But quietly left the Tram, made her way to the surface, flew down to the beach, followed the blue lights to the restored Odessan underground garden, and collapsed from exhaustion.

Kayli opened her eyes a day later, still in the garden, to Muncy saying, "Come on, little hero, it's time you were awake,"

Muncy helped the Sprite to a picnic table, then gave her a foot-long sausage and pepper hero and a tall glass of mint iced tea. Then said, "You look like crap,"

"I feel like it and probably sStevel like it too by now and thank you for the food. Oh, and please don't tell anyone that I was the one who found you,"

"You should get a pat on the back for what you did,"

Kayli took a bite of her grinder and said, "Do you really think people are gonna believe a foot-and-a-half tall Sprite rescued you? I don't think so,"

Steve sat on Muncy's right, gave her a kiss then said, "After what you went through. You should be home resting and not here cuddling this disgusting Sprite."

Muncy was about to tell Steve how she rescued her when Kayli slowly shook her head no.

Steve asked, "Hey, Dirtball, where were you when everyone was out looking for Muncy? Rolling in the mud somewhere? You know since you're not pulling your weight around here. I think I'll start a petition to have you removed from the Institute."

Kayli stated, "Off-worlders don't have that privilege, so back off with your threats,"

"Oh, that's a promise because all I have to do is talk to Tippy and tell her how you are a threat to the Institute's security, and you'll be off this planetoid before you know it."

Kayli stated, "You need proof,"

"I have proof. While you were on Earth, you disobeyed a direct order not to do anything to Greg, but you followed him, jeopardizing Muncy's life. That's not the only time you disobeyed a direct order. Do you remember when one of the prisoners escaped the Institute, and everyone was ordered to stay inside until he was caught? You blatantly disobeyed that order."

"I'm on Sprite Security which means I had the right to be outside," shouted a fuming Kayli.

Steve stated, "The bottom line is you are out to destroy Muncy any way you can,"

"That's not true," shouted Kayli, then hit Steve across the face with her hand, grabbed her grinder, and flew away.

Muncy turned to Stevel and said, "That was uncalled for."

"I'm only out to protect you, my Sweet,"

"And you still haven't answered me why you were leaving my home early one morning. Don't say you weren't because Mimi showed me the photo."

"Oh, that. Mimi got it all wrong; I wasn't leaving your home; I was checking the area to make sure things were secure,"

The following day Kayli entered Thor's office with Tippy and asked, "You wanted to see me, sir,"

Thor offered Kayli and his daughter coffee and a brownie and said, "Sit and relax; I'm waiting for one more person to show up for this hearing."

Kayli sat on the dark wooden mahogany chair with a pillow and could barely see above the top of the desk because of her short stature. Tippy sat Kayli on her shoulder, saying, "Just watch yourself with your coffee."

Kayli was almost finished with her brownie when Steve walked and stood on Thor's right side. Thor then stated, "This hearing will now come to order. Kayli, Steve has informed me about your insubordination and how you jeopardized Muncy's life several times, which will not be tolerated here at the Institute. Which means I could lock you up here at the Institute and throw away the key. Do you have anything to say for yourself, young lady?"

Kayli glared at Steve and thought, *"My goose is cooked no matter what I say in defense. So, I might as well take my punishment and wait for another day for the truth to come out.*" *Kayli then stated,* "No, Sir. There is nothing I can say in my defense, But I throw myself upon your mercy and receive whatever punishment you deem fit,"

Thor stated firmly, "As of this moment, you, Sprite Kayli Aubrette, will no longer work on Sprite Security. I will not allow you to live in your home on this planetoid. You will no longer be able to enter this area anymore because you are a security risk."

Tippy tried to say something in her defense, but Thor was firm on his Decision.

Kayli walked out of Thor's office with her head down, entered the Arboretum, and made her way back to the falls in the back right corner. Sat on the green grass on the left side of it and leaned against a tree. Let out a scream in frustration, then bellowed, "This is not fair, Lord. I didn't do anything to deserve this!" She looked up and saw General, the male security lion that stands five feet tall from the front paw to the top of his ear, slowly walking towards her with his head lowered.

Kayli softly muttered, "I'm Kitty Kibble for sure," Closed her eyes and waited for the lion's sharp teeth to mangle her little body. Instead, she felt the massive lion's tongue licking her face. General then laid down on the grass and nuzzled the sorrowing Sprite.

While Kayli was resting comfortably in the midst of the lion's massive paws, two men from security approached the lion to escort Kayli off the planetoid.

General instantly sprang to his feet and let out a long, loud roar forbidding them to touch the Sprite.

One man shouted, "General heel, we are not going to hurt you. We have to escort the Sprite off this planetoid,"

General lay back down, placed his paw on top of Kayli to protect her, then growled every time the men from security tried to get at Kayli.

Thor approached General to get him to release the Sprite, but the lion swiped at Thor's midsection with his massive paw.

Ruth approached the lion and stated in a soft voice, "We are not going to hurt your little friend Kayli. As a matter of fact, Thor has changed his mind, and she can stay on the planetoid and will continue her job on the Sprite security."

General stood and allowed Ruth to pick up Kayli, she then turned to her husband Thor and said, "General is protecting Kayli for some reason, and I think we should follow the lion's lead."

Kayli climbed on the lion's back, pointing, saying, "To my home General," She then stuck out her tongue at Steve as they passed.

All Steve could do was mutter, "Woah,"

A short time later, Kayli gave the lion a long hug. He then lay on her front porch to make sure no one was going to drag her away as she entered her home.

Sometime later, Muncy knocked on her front door, saying, "Kayli, you decent?"

Kayli rushed into the living room, flew up, and gave Muncy a hug, then said, "I'm not being kicked off this small rock of a planet and will keep my job. Yes!"

"I heard congratulations are in order on having General as your guardian and friend. Oh, hey, I came by to let you know that a bunch of us are getting together at the café this evening,"

"After everything that has happened, I think I'll stay home this tonight,"

Right after Muncy left, Steve boldly walked in and pointed his finger at Kayli, saying, "You are not going to get off that easy because as I live and breathe, you will not hurt Muncy again,"

Kayli glared up at Steve and asked, "What have you been smoking? Muncy is my friend,"

"So, you say," Steve left, then slowly walked by General, growling at him. He met Muncy talking to some of her friends a block from Kayli's, gave her a warm hug and kiss then entered into the conversation.

At Muncy's home, Steve took off his shirt and hollered, "Muncy, I need you to put some lotion on my back,"

"Can it wait? I'm trying to make some sense of my kitchen because it's a mess."

"No, now," demanded Steve.

When Muncy approached Steve with a tube of cream in her hand, he slapped her in the face saying, "Don't you ever talk back to me again. After you're finished with my back, fix me my evening meal."

"Yes, Sir." Stated Muncy somberly.

After Steve left late that night, Muncy thought, *"All Steve needs is a little love and prayer, and he'll soften."*

Early the next morning, Muncy walked to John *Bilmore*'s home three blocks away. When she entered, a man just under six feet tall with brown hair clad in white briefs was leaning against the hall wall in his white briefs said, "Welcome, stranger. Are you here to take care of me?"

Muncy smiled sheepishly and said, "Yes I'm your Home Health Aide, but I don't want to see you in your tidy whiteys while I'm here and the next time I come, be dressed,"

A spiteful John removed his underwear saying, "You're here as my home health aide so it's all right to see me naked."

Muncy turned her back saying, "You're making me feel uncomfortable please do that in the bathroom when you're ready for your shower,"

Some two minutes later, Muncy heard a crash, raced into the bathroom, and found John lying on the floor. She helped him to his feet, saying, "Please cover yourself while I'm in your presence because it's not right for me to see your bare butt."

Muncy sat him on a bench in the shower and said, "I am not going to wash your back or any part of you, you do that yourself,"

As Muncy turned to leave the bathroom, John asked, "How's Steve doing?"

Muncy paused as her demeanor took on that of a whipped dog and remained silent.

John said, "No matter what you do, you'll never change that overpowering, demanding attitude of his."

Muncy stated in mock innocence, "I don't know what you are talking about. Steve is sweet and kind. Now if you will excuse me, I have to make your morning meal,"

A short time later, John hobbled to the table clad in a dark blue robe, looked at Muncy and said, "You need a hug," and tried to wrap his arms around her. But she kept her arms stiff by her side, saying, "Please don't, and close your robe,"

John stated, "I don't know what Steve did to you, but you're gonna get a hug whether you like it or not."

While Muncy was wrapped in John's loving arms, all she could think of was how many times Steve raped her.

John asked, "Why are you trembling? I'm not going to force myself on you,"

Muncy broke free, changed the subject by saying, "You have to stay off those legs until they heal. Now sit and eat,"

"Yes, Mother," stated John smiling.

While John was eating, Muncy sat at the dining room table with him, took a swallow of her coffee and then said, "The next time your commander hollers, duck, you drop to the ground,"

"I thought he was telling us that a flock of Mallards were flying overhead, so I looked up and got nailed by an energy blast,"

After the morning meal, Muncy stated, "I'll help you dress but have your briefs on when I enter your bedroom,"

When Muncy was in the bedroom she sighed then rubbed the healing lotion on John's back and legs before she helped him dress.

He then asked, "What's wrong? You seem uncomfortable."

"I don't want to talk about it,"

"We will talk about it here and now,"

Muncy stated, "I am not going to talk about my personal life when you're in your underwear and don't you dare give me a hug,"

A persistent John stood, wrapped his arms around a trembling Muncy and asked, "Who hurt you,"

Muncy became hysterical thinking John was going to rape her and tried to break free from his loving arms but couldn't. She then looked in John's eyes, realized he wasn't going to assault her, put her head on his shoulder, and cried for five minutes.

After Muncy helped John dress and they were sitting on the bed, she stated, "One morning Steve broke in my home and assaulted me in the shower. I believe I can trust you," she showed John the red sores on her body and he gently touched her thigh saying, "Now I understand oh and nice legs. I have a cream that will help heal those sores can I rub it on you?"

There was something about John that made Muncy relax, she lay on the bed, in her pink brief and allowed John to rub a special red cream on her back.

An hour later, Muncy opened her eyes, sat up, kissed John, and helped him sit in his powerchair.

John asked, "Can you kneel close to me for a bit?"

When she did, John held Muncy's right hand, saying, "Thank for all you've done for me today, and I'll see you later,"

Muncy kissed John's lips saying, "No, thank you because I stopped being afraid of being attacked by men," and walked out of the bedroom.

John caught Muncy in the living room and asked, "Don't you think you should put your clothes on before you go outside,"

"Oh yeah, thanks."

7

Under attack

Every day for weeks Muncy was modest as she entered John's home and helped him with his daily activities. But today it didn't bother her when she greeted him in his lack of attire, but she smiled and gave him a long warm hug. Then joyfully attended to his needs in the shower by washing his back and wounded legs. After John's shower she happily walked him in the bedroom to dress, and didn't care that he was naked and asked, "Could you rub more of that cream on me? Because I like the results I got the last time."

John said, "Don't you think you should dress me first."

"I trust you," then lay on the bed in just her powder blue step-ins.

While Muncy was relishing every second John was applying the cream to her body, he inquired, "Will you please tell me how you got these nasty sores all over you?"

Muncy grew afraid to tell John that it was because of Steve. She felt a peace and stated, "I was sunning myself in my white string bikini in the privacy of my back yard. Steve approached me, didn't like how I was dressed and shot me I don't know how many times with something that stung like the Dickens."

After John applied the cream to Muncy's back, she rolled over saying with her arms outstretched, "Come here and give me a hug," then smiled when he passionately responded to her promptings and she was comforted by his love.

An hour later, Muncy woke, kissed John then said, "I am so sorry I maneuvered you to get in bed with me, but for the first time in months I enjoyed being with a man,"

John stated, "Actually I was looking for a way for us to snuggle totally dressed. But I liked your idea better. But I think we should abstain from intimacy until after the wedding. That's if you want to marry me."

"You're right. Sorry I got carried away by helping you in the shower."

As Muncy was leaving John's home, a four-foot-long mechanical Royal Blue Macaw landed on her shoulder. She glanced at him and asked, "What's up, Horatio,"

"If you are going to the Tram, don't because my scan picked up two men waiting for you there,"

"Have you told Thor and Sam yet?"

"I already have, and here they come now,"

Muncy caught their attention and said, "Hi Sam, Thor, you two out to kick some butts; mind if I tag along? They might be the ones who kidnapped me earlier,"

Thor and Sam entered the Tram; Muncy pointed to the man on the right dressed in jeans and a white shirt, saying, "He's the one who got fresh with me, which is putting it mildly, and the other guy beat me senseless,"

Thor asked the two men, "I'd like to see your planetary passes,"

The man on the right stated, "There is no such thing as planetary passes,"

"Yes there is, and you two will have to come with me,"

When neither one moved, Thor grabbed the one on the right saying, "You're a dead man for what you did to one of my employees and threw him off the Tram. He then landed three roundhouse kicks to his face sending him staggering backward. The man threw a punch at Thor's face; he caught his fist, twisted it, and broke his arm. Then landed another roundhouse kick to his face knocking him out.

Thor then shouted, "Hey Sam, how are you doing?"

"Great, here catch," and threw the man off the Tram.

Thor caught him by his sides, spun around, and threw him against a large boulder.

Muncy slowly approached the man who abused her; he looked at her and asked, "Yeah, what do you want," and stood to his feet.

Muncy stated, "This," and kicked him between his pockets, sending him to his knees in pain.

Thor put the two men on the Tram and said, "Muncy, take me to where these two roughed you up."

"Thor, Sir, actually, they boarded the Tram at King Mix's."

At King Mex's underground Tram Station, Thor and Sam dragged the two men into the station and then sent for the King.

Some eleven minutes later, a 40-inch-tall Sprite, clad in brown royal apparel with brown butterfly wings, entered the station, saluted Thor, and asked, "What is so important that you had to call me away from my fencing tournament."

"These two lowlifes have been using your Tram station as a means to gain access to this planetoid. I figured since this is your territory, you should be the one to decide what is to be done with them."

"I'll lock them up in my prison specially designed for humans; now move it, you two."

One man stated, "In your dreams, insects now get lost before I step on you."

Suddenly two dozen Sprite Archers entered the station, pointing their crossbows at the men. King Mex stated, "Move it or lose your life. The choice is yours, gentlemen."

A short time later, Muncy stared at the empty Tram, sighed then said, "Next stop Mary Bell Lake,"

At the lake, Muncy sat on the shore with her head down, thinking about what happened with John that morning. Steve tapped her shoulder, then slapped her across the face saying, "I don't want you to help that man again! If you do, there will be a lot more where that came from."

John needs someone to help him because of his injury, and Rose asked me to do it."

"I don't care what Rose told you to do; I'm telling you you're not going to help that man." He then belted her in the ribs.

John stepped out from behind a tall bush, using a four-foot-tall walking stick, saying, "I'll flatten you if you touch her again."

Muncy exclaimed, "John, how did you get here,"

"Remember, I'm on Thor's elite squad, which means I can move around this planetoid with ease. John grabbed Steve's right shoulder with his left hand, touched the pale blue retrieval button on his belt with his right, and vanished with him.

John returned eight minutes later, gave Muncy a hug, and said, "Steve's privileges of visiting this planetoid have ended. If he is seen around the Institute again, he will be shot."

Muncy stated, "You should not be walking on those legs because they're not healed yet. Go in my bedroom and get ready so I can put some of that healing cream on your hip and legs,"

That evening, Muncy was relaxing on her back deck enjoying a cup of hot Chamomile tea when John sat beside her and asked, "What bedroom can I sleep in?"

"What do you mean by that?" questioned a puzzled Muncy.

Thor told me that you needed protection, and I'm gonna make sure no one hurts you again,"

Muncy stated smiling, "I loved the way we mixed it up this morning and I wish you could sleep with me but it's wrong and we're not married so my bedroom is out of the question,"

"Our marriage has been all arranged, now come with me,"

"Hey, Mister Protector, you haven't asked me to marry you yet."

"Oh, will you."

Muncy muttered, "I have to think about marrying someone I've known for several weeks. I may regret this later on, but yes!"

The following day, Muncy was sitting at her mahogany dining room table dressed in her pink step-ins. Talking to her husband, John, clad in his white BVDs when in walked Sprite Kayli. She stared at them, put her hand over her eyes, saying, "My poor little eyes didn't just see what I think I saw."

Muncy stated, "Relax, Kayli, John and I are married, but give us a bit to get decent,"

"I turn my back for a minute, and you run off with the first thing in pants,"

"Kayli, how about a little support?" asked a shocked Muncy.

"Just kidding," stated Kayli, then flew and gave her a hugged,

John studied the gunk covering the Sprite and questioned, "What pray tell happened to you?"

"You know those huge three-inch long hard-shell bugs that fly around in groups? A bunch of us Sprites got together to do some Bug Bumping. But these bugs didn't like it and bumped us back big time. You should have seen what happened to Sprite Jed; he went to bump a bug but plowed right through it."

John laughed and said, "Sprite Jed came out clean, and your friends were splattered with bug innards."

"No, I was the only one who was splattered with bug juice,"

Muncy handed Kayli a bath towel saying, "You know where the shower is, and give me your clothes so I can wash them."

A short time later, Sprite Kayli lay on Muncy's country-style couch, wrapped in a blue bath towel, sound asleep. Muncy stared at her and then stated, "It's a shame the way she is treated just because she is eight inches shorter than all the other Sprites. But no one sees the spunk and energy she has. She didn't want me to say anything, but Kayli was the one who rescued me from those thugs. You know I bet Sprite Jed splattered Kayli on purpose, but there is no way anyone can prove it."

John stated, "Kayli is a lot like you, always getting the short end of things."

"Not to change the subject, did you get Thor's approval about going back to Earth to shut down Greg's drug business,"

"Yes, I got it first thing this morning."

"Good, I'll tell Cathy to find a temp for the Tram, and I'll pack. Oh, Kayli goes with us,"

"Okay, if you say so."

Sometime later, Muncy approached her husband and said, "Cathy can't get anyone to drive the Tram until tomorrow, so It looks like I'm it."

On the Tram halfway to Lake Mary Bell, Muncy hollered, "Ohmigosh," when she saw the tunnel was blocked. Then hollered, "Brace for impact! Computer, engage emergency reverse thrusters to full!"

Sometime later, Muncy stated, "Computer, emergency lighting," Then asked, "I need a head count."

Some of the eighteen Sprites on board moaned while the rest stated they were alright. Muncy asked, "Sprite Jed, get me the first aid kit Sprite Darlene is hurt bad, then check the others for injuries,"

"What happened," questioned Sprite Jed.

"There was a cave-in that blocked the Tram tunnel."

A short time later, Jed reported, "There are three Sprites with broken arms, one with busted ribs, and a whole bunch of bumps and bruises."

"Find something you can use for a splint and see if you can set those broken arms, then wrap something tight around the rib cage of the one with the busted ribs."

A nervous Jed asked, "Are we gonna die,"

Muncy stood and announced, "No one is going to die on my watch because I won't allow it, and the Rescue Squad should be here within the hour. If some of you have brought musical instruments for your picnic today, get them out and play something joyful and happy,"

Muncy looked at Sprite Darlene's scared demeanor, then said, "Sprite Jed, come here, sit and hold her in your arms and comfort her,"

Sprite Mist Ava with short brown hair, thirty-six inches tall, modestly dressed. Walked to Muncy, handed her a towel, and asked, "Did you know your head is bleeding? Sit in one of the seats, so I can patch you up."

Muncy roared back, "I'm in charge, so sit somewhere out of the way until we are rescued,"

Sprite Mist smiled, doubled up her fist, saying, "Do you want me to flatten you? If not, shut up and be quiet so I can tend to your wounds, and I don't want to hear another word out of you. Is that clear?" She then gave Muncy a hug and stated. "Thank you for taking care of us; now let me take care of you."

While Sprite Mist was bandaging Muncy's wound, Muncy said, "I take it you're a schoolteacher."

"That I am, and I'm used to dealing with Sprites who are obnoxious and rebellious."

"Could you take over for me? I'm not feeling so good,"

Sprite Mist hollered, "Listen up, everyone. Does anybody know what not to do in Bug Bumping?"

A male Sprite stood and said, "Make sure you're not flying fast when you bump a bug because it will be messy if you do,"

A female Sprite stood and stated, "Make sure you bump the bug with your hip and not your head. Because you may wind up kissing something you don't want to."

Sprite Mist asked, "Can anyone name the aerial activities sprites are active in."

Sprite Jed stood and stated, "There is Belly Skimming, where one flies low and skims the water with their belly. There is Tree Dodging, who can fly through a forest the fastest without smacking into a tree. There is Rock Racing; a Sprite runs to the bottom of the hill without the four-foot rock behind him, smushing him. Then there's Bug Bumping; the game is to bump the bug and fly away before the bug gets you. Then there is Log Rolling, which is similar to Rock Racing, but in Log Rolling, you have to fly low down the hill in front of a fast-rolling log and pray you don't smack into a tree or a rock before you get to the bottom. Then there is Wind Sailing; the trick is to see who Fly against a strong wind the longest without being blown against a tree."

When the rescue team arrived, and everyone was boarding the relief Tram, Muncy stopped Sprite Jed and said, "That wasn't nice of you splattering Kayli with bug entrails."

"I was just having some fun,"

"But Kayli has been the brunt of too many of the Sprite jokes, and it has to stop."

Jed muttered, "Grouch," as he walked away.

Muncy grabbed the Sprite by his shoulder, spun him around, and asked, "What did you just say?"

"Ah, nothing, ma'am,"

"I am not a grouch but concerned for Kayli. Since the Tram will be down for a few days, come with me to the gym."

In the gym twenty-three minutes later, Muncy pointed to Kayli, dressed in tight gold shorts and a halter top, rigorously engaged in Ninja exercises. Then stated, "The happy-go-lucky Sprite Kayli is now the dead serious Sprite bent on kicking the next person's butt who gives her a hard time."

Sprite Kayli approached Muncy and asked, "Can you get me another practice dummy? The one that I have been using suddenly exploded for some unexplainable reason. Oh, hi Jed,"

Sprite Jed swallowed hard, smiled sheepishly at Kayli then said, "Have I ever told you that you look great no matter what you are dressed in,"

Sprite Kayli glared up at Sprite Jed, got in his face, and said, "Big nasty Boo boos usually follow when a Sprite gets splattered with bug entrails. Remember that the next time we are Bug Bumping,"

Sprite Jed glanced at his watch, saying, "Will you look at the time? I have to be flying along before I am late for my next defense class."

After Jed was gone, Kayli fell to the floor, in side-splitting laughter for a good minute."

Muncy stated, "I see you haven't lost your sense of humor. So how are your morning exercises coming along,"

"My reflexes are getting better, and I think I'm developing good biceps. See."

Muncy knelt, put her hand on Kayli's shoulder, saying, "You know the Bible says that you are to forgive Spite Jed for what he did to you,"

"I know, and I'm working on it," Kayli took holed of Muncy's hand and flipped her on her Back.

A shaken Muncy stood, stared at Kayli in amazement then questioned, "How in the world did you get so strong,"

"Actually, I'm not a Sprite, but a Gnome from the Planet Pylee, and my people live in a deep fisher that is four thousand miles long call 'The Grave."

Muncy stated, "I have heard of the fantastic legends of the Pyleen Gnomes, and they had a gland in their bodies that gave them unlimited strength when needed, but they all died centuries ago,"

Kayli smiled and asked, "If they did, how do you explain me,"

"I can't, but there is one test that will prove who you really are. The Gnomes of Pylee could fly faster than sound. Can you?"

"The proof is in the pudding they say. What do you want me to do?"

"Lake Mary Bell is the only place a certain flower grows on rocks. Bring me one, rock and all,"

A short time later, Muncy stood on the shore of Smile Lake with Kayli and said, "Lake Mary Bell is eight hundred miles that way," pointed accost the lake, then said, "You have seven minutes to get me that flower."

Sprite Kayli shot skyward, and in a split second, she was gone, returning five minutes later carrying a foot-in-diameter rock with several flowers growing on it, gave it to Muncy and asked, "Is this what you were talking about."

8

A mole

In Muncy's home on Earth in Wickenburg, Arizona, she plopped herself on the couch and said, "Hubby of mine, this is my home away from home."

John sat on her right, saying, "I think I could get used to living on Earth,"

Kayli hollered, "I call first shower," and ran to the bathroom.

Some five minutes later, Kayli let go of a loud, terrifying scream; John raced into the bathroom and saw Kayli huddled in the corner of the shower, pointing at a huge brown Tarantula.

John took the small bathroom's wastepaper basket, scooped up the spider, placed a lid on it, and put it on the floor. Stared at a trembling Sprite still huddled in the corner of the shower. Wrapped her in a white bath towel and brought her into the living room.

Muncy asked, "What happened?"

"Some joker put a Tarantula in the shower, and Kayli happened to find it,"

"It takes a while for a Sprite to recover from something traumatic, so you'll have to hold her for a while. That's if you don't mind,"

John sat in the recliner with Kayli cradled in his arms, saying, "I don't mind; it's like having a little daughter."

Greg knocked on the sliding glass door, shouting, "Anybody to home?" Saw John with Sprite Kayli and said, "How about that, humans marrying Sprites, will wonders ever cease,"

"Get your mind out of the gutter Greg," stated John.

"You have me at a disadvantage. Whom might you be?"

"I'm Muncy's husband," stated John. "If you ever touch my wife in any way, I'll have you Keelhauled. Is that clear?"

"Yes, Sir," stated Greg sarcastically.

John said, "State your business, then leave,"

"What I have to say is for Muncy's ears only,"

"Then you have no business with my wife, so leave,"

As Greg went to walk to the bedroom, John put Kayli on the recliner and blocked Greg's path, saying, "What part of leave don't you understand,"

Greg landed a coward's punch to John's face knocking him to the floor. Kayli wrapped the towel around her, flew in Greg's face with her fist up, ready for action.

Greg went to swat her out of the way, but she quickly moved. Flew across the room, then towards Greg at one-eight the speed of sound, and landed on Greg's stomach, feet first, sending him flying backward into the fireplace. Kayli then called upon her reserved strength and dragged him outside. Then she stated, "You come in Muncy's home one more time, and I'll rip you apart."

"Big talk for a Sprite,"

"I'm not a Sprite but a Gnome from Pylee, and we are a force to be reckoned with."

Greg hollered, "Hey, Muncy, please put something on!"

When Kayli turned to look, Greg belted her in her chest, sending her flying into the stockade fence then left.

Muncy rushed to Kayli, and helped her up, asking, "Are you alright?"

"Yeah, but that's gonna leave a mark for sure,"

That evening the front doorbell rang; Muncy opened it and said, "Starlight and Nicholas Pawlet come in, come in; I haven't seen you two in a long time." Muncy then hollered, "Honey, we have company; put on the coffee,"

A short time later, Starlight took a swallow of her French Vanilla Coffee and then stated, "Now that you are in your right mind, hubby and I can head back home to HP5."

Muncy asked, "Do you want to expound on that, please."

"I'm not supposed to say anything, but Thor contacted us and told us to keep an eye on you because some of your actions earlier on Earth were pretty shady."

"Because a Neurotransmitter was injected in my arm, I had no control over my actions or recollection of what I did,"

"So, you say," stated a doubtful Nicholas.

"Come on, Starlight, we've been friends for a long time and have been through thick and thin together. Now tell me what I am supposed to have done that was so shady and underhanded,"

"Thor thinks you used the Neurotransmitter to act innocently while indulging in sex and drugs,"

"Then you two are just the ones to prove my innocence."

"How can we help," questioned Nicholas.

John stated, "First, we have to find Greg's contacts here on Earth."

Nicholas stated, "What you need is someone who Greg doesn't know to gain his confidence so he will spill the beans,"

Kayli walked into the living room clad in a skimpy two-piece green bathing suit and wearing Darlene's stardust ring to hide her wings and stated, "Instead of working on my tan, why don't I be the mole in Greg's organization and Nicklaus can be my contact,"

"Sounds like a plan," stated John, "So why don't you go to Greg's now before he hires someone else."

A short time later, a nervous Kayli knocked on Greg's front door in her bathing suit, praying he wasn't going to stomp on her.

Greg threw open the door, looked down at Kayli, and asked in a gruff voice, "Yeah, what do you want, imp."

"You need a courier, and I need money, so I think we can make a deal,"

Inside Greg's home, he brought Kayli into his back room which had futuristic computer equipment and told her to stand in the back right corner. When she did, a solid six-foot 3-dimensional image of her appeared on the other side of the room. Greg carefully examines every part of Kayli's image for any hidden bugs, microphones, cameras, or whatever. Pointed to her stardust ring and asked, "What is this?"

"That ring hides my Sprite wings while I'm here on Earth; the top half of my bathing suit has underwires so I can look perky."

"I'm okay with that. Now step behind the privacy curtain, take off your bathing suit, and lie on the cot because I need to do one more thing that computers can't do,"

A nervous Kayli knew what Greg was going to do and said, "I don't think this is going to work because I'm just a little bit of a thing,"

Greg pointed his energy pistol at her saying, "Ever since you showed up at Muncy's you've been trying to sneak into my home so you could report to Thor my dealings in drugs. If that is true, you're history,"

Kayli quickly stated, "I'm not here to snoop around so, let's get on with the tests,"

Some forty-three minutes later, Kayli looked up at Greg standing in front of her and stated, "Seriously, did we really have to do that because now I'm gonna be sore down there for a week,"

"I had to see how willing you are to obey and that was the only means I could think of. But before you put your bathing suit back on I want you to wear a dress that's lined with drugs. Then fly to 33 degrees fifty-eight point fourteen north and 112 degrees point 46.63 West. Stay there until your contact arrives."

"If the drugs are in my clothes, what am I going to wear once my contact has the drugs."

"I like your cute little bathing suit and it should be enough to fly back."

"The only time I wear this little thing is when I wanna get a tan in the privacy of my backyard."

"You can wear that cute little thing you call a bathing suit under your clothes, or you can go commando; I don't care just deliver the drugs. Oh, I'm having a get-together tonight at a secluded location. I would like you to be there so you can meet everybody, and don't forget to wear your tiny bathing suit."

A smiling Kayli stated, "Greg, before you put your clothes on, why don't you lie on the cot, so I can massage you the Sprite way,"

As Greg lay on his stomach, Kayli carefully walked up and down his body massaging it until he was asleep. She then covered him with a blanket and did some snooping in his office.

At the designated spot, Kayli gave her dress to a bearded man in a silver Humvee. He stepped out of his vehicle and stated. "No offense,

Little One, but this is just so you don't see which way we go," and hit Kayli knocking her out.

Sprite Jed stopped his bright red four-wheeler by an unconscious Kayli 47 minutes later. He placed his hand on her back and thought, "Her skin is way too dry. I'd better set up the treatment booth right away."

In less than five minutes, Jed had erected a four-square dark brown tent and hooked up a humidifier to it that sprayed a mixture of exotic oils. He then lay Kayli inside on a soft blue quilt face down, removed her bathing suit, and rubbed her down with a moisturizing cream before stepping outside.

Some 23 minutes later, Kayli set up and let go of a scream, then hollered. "The person who took off my bathing suit and messed around with me while I was unconscious is going to die."

Sprite Jed stated, "I took off your bathing suit so the oils and the moisturizer could penetrate every part of your body, and I didn't do what you think I did." He held a thin gray sheet inside the four-square dark brown tent saying, "Cover yourself with this so we can talk."

When Jed entered, Kayli set the sheet aside, saying, "I don't need to cover myself in front of you because you are my mate, which is something I want to talk to you about."

"But first I need to check your skin to see if the moisturizing treatment is working," and placed a round metal gage on her stomach, back and limbs then stated, "Another twenty minutes should do it." Jed then shouted, "If I didn't come along when I did you would have been a dried out corpse baking in the desert heat."

"I had to make an important delivery."

"You know as well as I do that a Sprite's body will dehydrate in desert heat until there is nothing left but some crispy remains."

Kayli stated, "Back to what I wanted to talk to you about. Some five months ago, we signed all the proper papers and became mates before a pastor, yet you treat me as an outcast. Why?"

"You isolate yourself from everyone and do weird things that none of us sprites understand. Yes, I agreed to be your mate, but I have second thoughts."

"You are ashamed of me because of my short stature, and that is why you constantly tease me and make fun of me in front of the other

Sprites. I did not exactly like being splattered with bug innards, but I try to understand and forgive you."

Jed stated, "I was thinking of reversing our commitment to each other so you could be free and find another Sprite."

"I will not release you from your commitment to me. You are my mate, and I am yours, like it or not. Oh, here is something I should've told you when we fell in love. I am not a Sprite but a Gnome from the caverns of Pylee. That's why I stay by myself because I don't want the other Sprites to know who I am, and a Gnome's skin will not dry out in the desert heat. Now get ready to consummate our relationship, and if you don't want to, I'll mess you up really bad." Kayli then took off Jed's shirt, saying, "We can do this the easy way or the hard way."

An hour later, a happy Jed finished packing the four-wheeler; Kayli approached him and hugged his left arm, saying, "Snuggling with me wasn't so bad, was it."

"It was the worst day of my life. Just kidding." He picked Kayli up, held her

in his arms, saying, "As a human would say, "You, wife of mind, are gonna be in big trouble when we get home because I want to make up for lost time."

"Kayli smiled, saying, "Yes!" She then said, "I have to attend the shindig that Greg is throwing tonight, and he requires me to wear this little thing. Sorry."

Jed stopped the four-wheeler, held Kayli saying, "I can't live without you, and I promise I won't leave your side,"

A sorrowful Kayli held Jed tight, saying, "I hated doing certain things to get on Greg's good side but I had no choice,"

"Believe me, I understand and am aware of Greg's track record with the feminine gender, and I know about the test with him on the cot you had to do in order to get him to trust you,"

A relieved Kayli stated, "Then you know I had to snuggle with him. Oh, can you drop me off at Nicklaus's place because he is driving me to the party,"

At Greg's party, Kayli had all she could do to keep the men's hands off her as she flew around serving drinks. Then halfway through the party, she spotted a cloaked figure standing alone in a corner. She flew to it and whispered, "Cathy l Loganberry, what are you doing here?"

"Thor had me check out a meeting that involved a lot of top businessmen, and I was ushered through a portal to this party." Cathy nervously glanced around, then said, "Some of the ones here are on Thor's Most Wanted List,"

Kayli stated, "Meaning, if they see you, you're dogmeat."

"Exactly, and what are you doing here dressed like a common streetwalker?"

"I'm working under the covers,"

"You mean undercover,"

"Yeah, that too, and I have an idea how to get you out of here without turning you into toast, and that is to turn you into Greg; then I'll do my thing," Kayli pushed Cathy into the light shouting, "Hey everyone, look who I found skulking around in the shadows,"

Greg walked up to Cathy, belted her in the face saying, "Good work Kayli,"

Kayli asked, "May I have the honor of killing her?"

"Sure,"

Kayli picked up a silver serving tray, spun around, hitting Cathy across her face, and sending her to the floor out cold. Then said, "What I'm gonna do to her next is too gruesome to watch,"

A fat man approached Kayli and said, "How do we know you won't release her once you're out of our sight,"

Kayli drew on her reserved strength, picked him up by his belt, and threw him across the room, then asked, "Anyone else want to challenge me?"

Once outside, Kayli put Cathy in the back seat of Nicklaus's car, saying, "Bring her to Muncy, then bring me her clothes and a recording of a woman screaming,"

When Kayli had what she asked Nicklaus to bring, she played the recording and blasted the clothes with her energy ring. Dragged the smoldering clothes to Greg and said, "Is this proof enough that I mean what I say,"

Greg picked Kayli up, and sat her on his shoulder, shouting, "Give it up for Kayli The Brave, who killed one of The Galaxy Sentinel's main men!"

At Muncy's home, Kayli took a long hot shower, dressed in her beige slack suit, then sat under a large bush in the right corner of the backyard. Hung her head, saying, "Gracious Heavenly Father, I am so thankful for the finished work on the cross of Christ that I can stand in your presents clean and righteous. Right now, I feel like crud because I had to cuddle with a human man, Greg, If it were up to me, I would go back to the caves on Pylee and hide there. But I'm a mole in Gregg's organization and need to shut him down, which means I need your help to go forward to finish my task. Thank you for your peace and you're understanding."

Muncy sat on Kayli's left and said, "The only time you set here is when you're upset."

"I'm in tight with Greg and his cronies, which means I had to do some not-so-nice things, so he made me his Valet girl. This means I have to attend to him personally, which is something I do not want to do, but I have to in order to shut this drug operation down."

Muncy inquired, "Can you tell me what Greg does to the women who are injected with a neurotransmitter?"

Kayli's face lost all expression when she said, "Trust me, you don't want to know."

"Yeah, I do,"

"When the neurotransmitter is activated, it overrides the person's will to resist, and they becomes a human automaton. So, all the while the neurotransmitter was in your arm, you performed any task Greg asked you to do." Kayli Padded Muncy's stomach saying, "I see you don't have a bun in the oven, which is a good thing seeing the length of time that neurotransmitter was in your arm."

A shocked Muncy asked, "You're kidding me? Please tell me that I was not in bed with Greg,"

"Sorry, but I am not kidding because the sexy pictures Greg took of you were not taken by that camera he hid on the fence but in his home. So, you were in bed with Greg quite often,"

Muncy stated, "I think I'm gonna be sick because I don't remember doing that."

"Oh, the best part is he had you attend his shindigs wearing some thin, slinky see through dress for his male guest's pleasure."

Muncy stated, "Overload, overload, overload, which is way more information than I wanted to hear."

Kayli hung her head, saying, "I know this because I was in your shoes without the neurotransmitter."

Muncy grew silent as she stared at the Gnome then asked, "How were you able to hold up emotionally?"

"It still bothers me, and have trouble sleeping,"

In the house, Kayli stared up at John and asked, "Daddy John, can you hold me for a while?"

John sat in the recliner, with Kayli in his lap, she curled up, and went to sleep.

9

Kayli to the rescue

The next morning, Kayli was enjoying her scrambled eggs with bacon. Took a swallow of her Chamomile tea, then said, "Muncy, as you know I am Greg's personal valet and Mister Silk Undies wants to talk to you today at eleven o'clock, and he wants you to wear something frilly."

Muncy stated, "In other words, the enemy wants me to be dressed to the nines."

"You got it,"

Muncy gave John a kiss then said, "If I'm not home in an hour, come rescue me,"

Exactly at eleven, Kayli announced, "Sir Greggory, Muncy is here to see you."

Kayli flew in front of Muncy clad in a long fancy black dress that went down to her ankles, led her into the den and closed the door.

Greg was dressed in a blue three-piece suit, sitting in a comfortable black leather chair by the fireplace. Put his ivory pipe on a small metal table on his right, stood, and greeted Muncy. She smiled politely then stated, "Can the formalities Creep, state what you want me for so I can get on with the rest of my life."

"You took something from me, and I want it back."

Muncy snapped back, "You took something from me too, so we are even,"

"I took nothing from you!" shouted Greg.

"You stole I don't know how many months from me by the way of your neurotransmitter and abused me in ways I don't care to discuss."

Feeling guilty Greg asked, "How do you know what I did? Did my valet tell you?"

"Duhhh, a moronic woman could have figured out what you did to her by your actions. You like wild parties, and loose women, which says you would have indulged in your flesh with her multiple times. Oh, I woke up one morning wearing deep pink lipstick, and I hate that color and another morning I woke like I just came from the shower. Do you want me to go on?"

Greg approached Muncy, stood a foot from her, then ripped off her dress in anger.

Muncy asked smiling, "Surprised I wore Bermuda shorts and a halter top under my rip away dress?"

"Where did you hide the drugs; you stole from me?" screamed Greg.

"Go to Planet PX-12 in the Blue Ringed System. When you enter the cave, walk straight until you see a long ledge on your left. Follow that ledge until you see a large black boulder blocking your way. Look to your left and you will see a crack in the cave wall, the drugs are in there."

Greg took an energy pistol from inside his suit coat, pointed it at Muncy saying, "Now that I know where the drugs are you are no longer useful to me."

But before he could fire his pistol, Kayli flew in his face knocking him backward. Causing the energy blast to be deflected off a large mirror then bounced off a shiny bronze statue that struck Greg, vaporizing him.

A thankful Kayli plopped herself in the comfortable chair saying, "It's over,"

Muncy stated, "No it's not, we need to take down the other drug couriers and the King Pin behind the operation," she picked up Kayli saying, "You need some timeout in a hot tub."

Later, Kayli was relaxing in her personal hot tub in her tiny bikini in the back right corner of the backyard when a shadow loomed over her. She muttered, "Whoever you are, you wanna move to the left because you're blocking my sun,"

When the person didn't move, a frustrated Kayli stated, "I said move your miserable hide!" She then looked up and screamed, "Steve, what are you doing here,"

Steve shoved Kayli's head under the water and held it there for almost a minute, picked her up and asked, "Where's Muncy?"

Gasping for air, Kayli stated, "I don't know, in the house I guess."

"I checked and she isn't there, now where is she?" demanded Steve.

"Then she's probably out with her husband John. You wanna let go of my body so I can get out?"

Steve refused to let Kayli get out of the hot tub saying, "What do you know about Greg's death,"

"He was being stupid with Muncy and tried to shoot her, missed and the energy blast, ricocheted awesome mirror, then office statue then hit and killed him."

"That's your story, but what really happened,"

Kayli wiggled out from under Steve's grasp, flew to the pic nick table, wrapped a towel around her saying, "So I say because I was Greg's personal valet."

"If you were, then what is the access code to his computer?"

"The date of his birthday. Greg got up every morning at six sharp, worked out for an hour in his skivvies, then pinched my sit-down before he showered for forty-five minutes. He wore silk undies and PJs and had a main squeeze by the name of Kathleen Star. Oh, Greg snores like an atlas five rocket, sleeps on his back and has a reoccurring dream about an Earth woman by the name of Callie Swanson from Spokane, Washington."

"What is going to happen to Greg's equipment?" asked Steve.

"The Galaxy Sentinel will be here either today or tomorrow to confiscate it."

"I heard you took out Cathy Loganberry. Is that true,"

"Roasted her sit-down is more like it."

Steve stared at Kayli for a few seconds, then said, "Kayli, bravest of the brave. You did something no one else could do and that is take out one of Thor's top men. That's all well and good, but now you work for me. To start, I want a back rub."

"You have to key to Greg's place, go in the bedroom, get ready but leave your undies on, and I'll be in shortly. Oh, you touch me in any way, you are history."

"Big talk from someone who is barely over two feet."

Kayli drew upon her reserved strength, lifted one end of the picnic table saying, "I am not all talk, but I follow through with my threats. One more thing, I will not perform or wear any sexy thing for you or your guest."

After Kayli walked up and down Steve's bare back massaging it for an hour. She put her towel back on and sat with him on the bed with him staring at her saying, "By that look in your eyes you want sex, which means I'm in big trouble. Go in the backroom where Greg has a device that will transform me into a six foot being, then we can get into it,"

In Greg's backroom, Kayli stood in the back right corner of the room, a solid six-foot 3-dimensional image of her wearing a skimpy bikini appeared lying on the cot on the other side of the room. Kayli hid then said, "You can come in now,"

Steve entered, stared in amazement at a shapely six foot Kayli. But when he began to kiss the three-dimensional image of her. She opened a two dimensional portal where he was and sent him to the busy metropolis of Posa City which is the Main city of Planet Avalon Prime.

Kayli turned off the scanner saying, "That's payback for what you did to me last year on Smile Lake Beach."

Just then a portal opened and a six foot tall, man with deep brown hair, rugged looking walked out. Stared at Kayli in her skimpy attire and asked, "Why are you running around with barely anything on?"

Kayli snapped to attention saying, "Sorry, Thor Sir, I was enjoying myself in a hot tub when Steve interrupted me and almost drowned me while he was interrogating me. So, I brought him here to give him a back rub then sent him to Posa City in his underwear."

Thor knelt, hugged Kayli then said, "I've heard what you been doing as Greg's valet. As far as I'm concerned that's going above and beyond the call of Duty."

The tearful Gnome asked, "Can I go back being just Kayli? Because I don't know how much more I can take of this underworld life and now Steve wants me to be his personal Valet."

Thor sat on the floor, leaned back against the outer wall, held Kayli in his arms saying, "I need a verbal report of what you've been doing and leave nothing out,"

Some twenty four minutes later, Thor stared at a smiling Kayli and asked, "Feel better?"

"Yeah, like a weight has been lifted off my shoulders,"

"That's good, now put something on because the guys from the lab are gonna be here any minute to catalog all this junk."

The portal opened and Rose walked out, stared at her husband holding Kayli and asked, "Indulging in extramarital activities with a Sprite?"

Thor let Kayli go, stood saying, "Just doing some one on one counseling. Where are the men from the lab?"

"The way Kayli is dressed I'd say you were doing a one on one snuggling if you ask me, and the men from the lab will be here shortly,"

Kayli stated, "Rose, Ma'am, we weren't osculating, or into touchy feely. Thor was helping me because of all the garbage I had to do as an undercover Gnome."

Rose smiled saying, "I know, I was just giving him a hard time. Do you want me to help you get dressed,"

"Could you please,"

Later, Rose took Kayli to Chaparral Homemade Ice Cream and Kayli ordered a banana split while Rose ordered a chocolate sundae. Then said to Kayli, "What you've done so far is amazing for someone your size. But Thor needs you here until all the drug lords are rounded up."

"As long as I don't have to mess around in bed with a human male, I'll do it. But don't worry I don't have a bun in the oven because Humans and Gnomes are incompatible, thank the Lord,"

Rose asked, "And what is that supposed to mean?"

An ashamed Kayli looked down and said, "In order to gain Greg's confidence I had to perform certain tasks and one of them was ah, letting him try to make me a mommy and if I didn't let him he was going to kill me,"

Rose stated, "You poor thing. I won't force you into taking down the rest of the drug couriers because you've suffered enough."

"Thanks, but I'm alright,"

Outside Kayli saw a young man clad in old jeans and a tattered t-shirt harassing a woman. Walked to him and said, "Hey Meat Head, the lady said to leave her alone, so, take a powder,"

The young man laughed, then said, "Beat it bug before I step on you."

Kayli kicked him in his shin saying, "Leave her alone, or I'll stomp all over your miserable hide."

The young man hit Kayli in the face knocking her to the asphalt, she sprang to her feet, jumped up, took hold of his pants, and swiftly climbed up to his neck. Held his shirt collar in her left hand called upon her reserved strength and continually slammed her fist in his face until he lay on the asphalt bloodied and screaming in pain. As the young man was walking away, Kayli let go a scream, ripped one of the small bushes out of the ground and threw it at him, knocking him down.

The woman knelt, thanked Kayli then asked, "What are you,"

She smiled saying, "I got tired of all the bullies harassing people, so I worked out until my muscles had muscles.

After the crowd left, a young woman hollered, "Someone please help me! I locked my keys in the car, and I can't get my baby out."

Kayli approached the woman and asked, "Can I help?"

A well-built man in his thirties chuckled than said, "This is a man's job kid,"

Kayli stated, "Just for grins and chuckles, let me have the first shot at breaking the driver's side window."

The man glanced a Kayli then hammered at the window for a good minute but couldn't break it then said, "Knock yourself out kid," holding his tender right hand.

The woman lifted Kayli up, she let go a scream and drove her fist threw the window then looked at the man saying, "Wimp,"

The man stated, "I weakened it for you,"

Kayli went to the rear of the SUV, pointed to it saying, "Pick it up,"

"Are you nuts? I can't pick up five thousand pounds,"

Kayli stared at the man saying, "Weakling," and lifted the back of the car with ease.

The man looked at Kayli holding up the back of the car with his mouth opened in shock then said in unbelief, "It's a trick, someone your size can't possibly pick that car up,"

Kayli put the SUV down and asked, "Can I feel your muscles?"

The man knelt saying, "Sure,"

Kayli gently placed her hand on his bicep, saying, "That's mush," and squeezed causing the man to cry out in pain.

10

The plan

Back at Muncy's home, an emotionally exhausted Kayli poured herself an iced tea and then flew to the top of the nearest tree. She slowly sipped her tea and wondered how she was going to make it through the next few months because she was forced to be intimate with Greg. Then she said, "Gracious Heavenly Father, Thank you for the finished work of the Cross." but before Kayli could tell the Lord about how she was still emotionally distraught because she had to get in bed with Greg. A quiet stilling peace flooded her, washing away all the hurt and memory of it,"

Jed flew down, lit on her right side, and said, "With the amount of smoke coming from this tree, I thought it was on fire, but it was just you thinking."

Kayli fell into Jed's arms, saying, "Boy, am I glad you are here,"

"What kind of trouble did you get yourself into this time?"

"I have to help take down the drug operation, and I am running on empty."

"Don't fret none because Thor sent me to help you take down the lowlifes on Earth."

"Great, I'm the boss, and you are my stud muffin, ah second in command."

"What's the game plan?"

"First, we go to Greg's place and soak in his hot tub in sans clothes until we are white and wrinkly. Then we'll slip between the silk sheets of his bed and try to put a bun in the oven,"

"Do you have a plan B?"

"Sure do, but it's a repeat of plan A,"

About two days later, a tattered Kayli and Jed walked in the sliding glass door to Muncy's home smiling. She stared at the disheveled diminutive couple and asked, "Good Lord, what in the world happened to you two?"

Kayli rubbed Jed's right arm, saying with a smile, "My mate Jed has returned to me. So, we made up for lost time,"

Say no more but get yourselves cleaned up for Supper. Then we have to figure out who and how we are going to catch Greg's other cronies."

After the Supper of roast beef, mashed potatoes, mushroom gravy, and corn on the cob, they sat in the living room, and Kayli stated, "The ones we have to catch are Big Tony, Tiny Malone, Steve Thomson, The Twins, and Dunkin. These guys are like Greg; they're just carriers who transferred the drugs to make sure the alliance can't track them once they get back to our side of the Galaxy."

Muncy made a pot of coffee to be served with the apple pie. John called the meeting to order and said, "We need a foolproof plan to take down these men. Does anyone have any ideas?"

Muncy stated, "Big Tony likes his women slim and sexy, but who are we going to get."

Jed swallowed a fork full of his apple pie, stared at Muncy, saying, "You fit the bill, but we need some drugs for Bate,"

Kayli stated, "As Gerg's valet, I know where he stashed the drugs, and he has a pile of it,"

Muncy waved her hands in front of her, saying, "Absolutely not. The Lord may have blessed me with a great-looking body, but I am not going to flaunt it in front of some sex-craving maniac,"

John stated, "Kayli, we'll need about two kilos to tantalize Big Tony. Then you, Kayli, follow him to where he makes the drop-off. That's when we nab him."

Nicklaus stated, "We need a backup plan just in case something goes wrong."

Some two days later, Muncy put on a hot pink, low-cut strapless sundress, splashed herself with her favorite perfume, picked up the drugs, and headed out the door.

On a desolate part of Kellie Road, Wickenburg, Arizona, Muncy got out of her car and handed Big Tony a satchel full of drugs. He dropped the satchel and held Muncy in his arms, kissing her.

Muncy stated, "I'd like to continue, but someone might come by and see us in the middle of things."

But Big Tony wouldn't listen to Muncy and kept kissing her to the point she became distressed, trying to keep him from handling the merchandise.

Kayli was hiding in a large bush nearby and stated over her computer watch, "John. We go to plan B because Muncy's in big trouble,"

When no one answered her, she flew skyward, straight for Big Tony, and slammed into his head, saying, "Hey, what's the big idea making out in the middle of my flight path? So, move it, you, Big Lummox," Kayli spotted the leather bag by Big Tony, flew down, and opened it, saying, "Do you have some goodies in here? She then stated, "Oooo, bags of pretty blue powder. Can I have one,"

An irritated Tony stopped kissing Muncy and ripped the bag out of the Gnome's hands, saying, "That is Stardust and not for Sprites,"

"Is that the hallucinatory drug the humans are raving about?"

"Yes, and it belongs to me,"

Muncy lifted her dress and took an energy pistol from the holster strapped to her right thigh, saying, "Big Tony, by the powers invested in me by the Planetary Alliance, I arrest you for drug trafficking and sexual assault. Kayli, open a portal to the Institute and inform Thor,"

With Big Tony safely tucked away, Kayli approached Muncy and asked, "Are you alright?"

"Outside of being emotionally shaken up because of my encounter with big Tony, I'm okay," Muncy spoke in her computer watch, "I have a pickup at my position."

Kayli flew and landed on Muncy's head, looked around, and asked, "Where do you suppose John and Jed are? They were our backup but are nowhere to be seen."

Just then, a tall man clad in blue dress pants and a white shirt walked up to Muncy and said, "Afternoon Ma'am. Are you sure you want to be out here by yourself? Because you never know who you're going to meet,"

"I'm fine, but thanks for your concern," stated Muncy.

The man stuck a revolver in her stomach, saying, "Hand over the loot, and you won't be hurt,"

The man looked down when Kayli kicked him in his shin, saying, "It's not nice to point things at people, especially if it's an old archaic weapon."

The man looked back at Muncy, pointing her energy pistol at his face and saying, "Hit the road before you are micro dust," then vaporized a nearby cactus. Then stunned him and turned him over to the police.

A long time later, Muncy glanced at her watch, saying, "John's instructions were to wait here for them after Big Tony was arrested, and that was two hours ago."

A man on a deep red motor scooter stopped, gave Muncy a note, then left. She opened the note and read, "You may have Big Tony, but I have John and Jed; come to 190 East Cavaness Avenue so we can talk."

Some forty minutes later, Muncy knocked on the door of 190 East Cavaness Avenue. Steve opened it, Muncy and Kayli entered, and Muncy demanded, "Release my husband and Jed right this minute,"

"Steve stated, "You don't have the right to demand anything, and I am in the position to grant you nothing. Tiny Malone, Steve Thomson, The Twins, and Dunken returned to the Planetary Alliance so that they wouldn't be turned over to the Galaxy Sentinel now I want Kaylee as my valet. If not, I'll kill John and Jed."

Kayli stated, "Okay, I'll be your nose wiper,"

Muncy shouted, "No, Kayli, don't do it because he's bluffing,"

"Am I?" questioned Steve. Then showed John and Jed on a flat screen, standing in front of a river of lava with their hands and feet tied. Then said, "One word from me and their history. So, what is it going to be, Kayli? If you say yes, they live if you say no, they die,"

As soon as Kayli agreed, John and Jed walked out of a portal with sweat running down their faces.

Kayli kissed Jed, then said, "I release you from your commitment to me as my mate because I'm not gonna come out of this alive."

A sobbing Jed stated, "I don't wanna hear that negative talk coming out of your mouth."

"If a miracle does happen and I come out of this in one piece, I won't be fit to be called your mate because my duties I performed for Steve," With her head lowered, Kayli approached Steve and said, "I'm yours,"

Steve stated, "That wasn't very nice of you to send me the poster city in my underwear. So be nice or I'll return the favor,"

As Muncy, John, and Jed were leaving the house, they heard Steve say, "Kayli, I need to take a shower, so get yourself ready to help me in there, and if you say no, I'll vaporize you where you stand."

A short time later, at the Al Ranchero Restaurant, Muncy ordered the Mexican salad with coffee, John ordered the Chille Relleno with coffee, and Jed ordered the Burrito Light with tea. Muncy asked, "How are we gonna get Kayli away from Steve?"

John answered, "We're not because Steve is holding all the cards right now."

"We have to do something," stated Muncy.

"If we try and rescue Kayli right now, he'll kill her or come after one of us so, the safest place for her is right where she is,"

Jed took a sip of his tea and said, "Kayli isn't wrapped too tight right now because of what Greg did to her. If we leave her in the hands of Steve, who knows what she'll do,"

John stated, "We'll just have to pray,"

Sprite Darlene walked into the restaurant, sat on Jed's left, gave him a peck on his cheek, and asked, "Where's your little main squeeze, Kayli,"

"She's working undercover,"

"Don't you mean she's working under some guy's covers?"

An angry Jed said, "State your business, then leave,"

"Can't. Thor sent me here to replace the way word, Gnome Kayli," stated Darlene, smiling.

Jed placed his hand on Darlene's back, slowly rubbing it, then stopped when his hand was between her wings and pinched a nerve that sent a sharp pain through her body, causing her to scream.

The manager approached her and said, "I'm gonna have to ask you to keep it down or leave."

Jed glared at Darlene, saying, "You say another derogatory word about Kayli, and you'll be walking for a while if you keep it up,"

"You wouldn't dare do that to my wings,"

Jed then pinched a nerve between Darlene's wings, causing them to go limp against her back. Then smiled and questioned, "What's the big idea coming in here with your wings exposed,"

"I tell everyone that I'm attending a cosplay, and they believe me, and what did you do to my wings?"

"There are nerves on a Sprite's back that will cause great pain or make the wings go limp for an hour when they are pinched, and that's what I did to you. Now, please tell me why all the Sprites are against Kayli?"

"She's a stupid Gnome who likes crawling around in dark caves, for crying out loud,"

Jed's anger burned within him because of what Darlene was saying about his mate, but he held it in. Then a vindictive Jed gently rubbed Darlene's back, saying, "I am sorry I pinched that nerve," then pinched her bra strap, unhooking it.

An embarrassed Darlene quickly wrapped her arms across her chest, saying, "Hey Creep, which wasn't a very nice thing to do to me; now I'm gonna have to go in the woman's room and try and hook it."

"It's not nice what you were saying about Kayli,"

Darlene stuck her chest out saying, "Why don't you dump that cave crawler and hook up with a real woman Sprite, like me."

Jed stood with his fist clenched by his side and glared at Darlene. She thought he wanted to kiss her and stood with her arms stretched towards him. Instead, Jed cold-cocked Darlene, then smiled as he watched her eyes roll back and slowly collapse on the floor out cold.

John stated, "There was no reason to hit her even though she was a pain in the neck with her nasty comments about Kayli."

Jed picked up Darlene, put her back in her chair, and patted her head as if to say he still liked her.

When Darlene opened her eyes, she muttered, "Gnome Lover,"

Jed pointed to the floor saying, "You lost something," and picked up her bra.

Darlene grabbed it out of his hand saying, "Creep,"

John said, "What we need to do is go after Steve. But this time, we do it unconventionally. In other words, we throw out the Planetary Alliance's rules."

Muncy stated, "What if we kidnap Kayli, then trick Steve into going to Area 51 in search for her, but we make sure he has an energy pistol on him? This way, Steve won't be coming back."

Jed stated, "That's kinda mean don't you think."

Muncy stated, "If it were up to me, I'd castrate him, then feed him to the sharks."

"Not too ticked off at Steve, are you." Stated John.

Weeks later, Kayli was walking past a church on West Apache Street when Jed approached her from behind and said, "Hey, Sweet cheeks, haven't seen you in weeks. What have you been doing,"

"Bug off,"

"I don't see any bugs on you,"

"I work for Steve, and I'm not allowed to talk to the likes of you."

Jed whispered in his computer watch, "Now,"

A US army van screeched to a halt; the side sliding door opened, and a man in military garb grabbed Kayli and sped away,"

Jed screamed, "Hey, you can't do that! Come back here with my mate!"

Some five minutes later, Jed's computer watch sounded. He answered it, saying, "Steve, you old Dog. How's business?"

"What did you do to Kayli,"

"Did your snitch tell you that the US put the snatch on Kayli for some strange reason? And by the looks of the van, I'd say someone in Area 51 wanted her."

"Stay right where you are. I'll be there in ten minutes,"

Some nine minutes later, Steve brought his BMW to a screeching halt, jumped out of the car, ran up to Jed, and shouted, "Tel me to my face. What did you do to Kayli?"

Jed stated, "I told you the US Army took her; if you don't believe me, believe the video I took."

After Steve saw the video, Jed asked, "What's wrong? You look troubled,"

"Kayli was the only drug Courier; all the others went back to the Alliance to hide for fear of The Galaxy Sentinel."

Jed smiled, saying, "In other words, the big boss will want some answers you don't have the answers for."

"You don't know the half of it,"

While Jed was talking to Steve, a portal opened behind him and slowly moved toward him until it enveloped him, Jed spoke into his computer watch, "We got him."

Muncy stated over the computer watch, "Drive the car back to Steve's place and wrap things up."

Jed stated, "Now the fun begins trying to locate the big boss. Oh, and How's Kayli?"

"Unusually quiet."

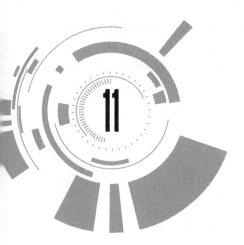

11

Rescue Steve

Back at the Institute, on the other side of the galaxy, hidden in an asteroid field called The Rockpile. Muncy and John rested in their home while Jed approached Kayli on Smile Lake Beach, sunning herself in light tan shorts and a white halter top. Asked, "Shall we pick up where we left off when we were on Earth?"

"Can you give me time to recuperate from Steve? Then we can take a stroll on the beach, if you want, or share a malt in the cafeteria,"

Jed gave Kayli a friendly hug, then said, "I'm gonna take the tram to Lake Mary Bell to get away from the Institute; you wanna join me?"

"For now, this is as far as I want to go,"

At Lake Mary Bell, Jed changed into his bathing suit and was about to romp in the water when he heard, "Don't get your wings wet."

He turned around, and there, clad in a pink string bikini, was Darlene smiling at him. She then asked, "Where's your cave crawler?"

"She's exhausted,"

Darlene smiled sinisterly, then stated, "Don't let Kayli's sweet smile and her shapely figure fool you. I know for a fact Gnomes prefer humans over their own kind for a mate, and that's why she went after Greg and Steve, and that is why she is so tired."

"But Kayli told me that humans and Gnomes are incompatible when it comes to sex."

"Don't let that silver-tongued devil fool you; she's probably worn out because she is expecting Steve's baby,"

"But Kayli doesn't lie or fool around,"

Darlene touched Jed's back, saying, "I have never met a Gnome who told the truth. In other words, a Gnome's idea of truth and ours are different. Now, how about a kiss,"

"But that might lead to other things."

"So, what if it does,"

Jed sighed, then said, "You're right; Kayli has been stringing me along. But I don't know about kissing you in public,"

Darlene smiled, saying, "I know of a hidden cave where we can have all the privacy we want."

An hour later, Jed was walking out of the cave with Darlene hanging on his right arm. They bumped into Kayli, glaring at them with her arms folded across her chest.

Jed quickly stated, "I can explain,"

"No, you can't, so don't even try because the smile on Darlene's face tells me what you two were doing. I flew here to tell you that Thor wants to know where your report is, and I find you mixing it up with Miss Floozie."

Kayli called upon her reserved strength, picked up a four-foot-in-diameter boulder, and tossed it in the lake. They stared at Darlene, saying, "Don't cross me, or you'll be under the next one." She flew skyward and was gone in seconds.

An emotionally devastated Kayli landed face down on her front lawn with her clothes smoldering because of the speed at which she flew. Gideon Bear patted her head, then handed her a note that read, "Are you going to work out in the gym today? Because I want to use the gym to work on one of my skits," Cathy said.

In the gym eleven minutes later, Cathy approached Kayli, beating the daylights out of a practice dummy, and asked, "What in the name of the Planetary Alliance happened to your clothes? They look like they've been in a fire,"

"I flew too fast after I caught Jed cheating on me, and this is the result,"

Cathy smiled, saying, "You're pulling my leg; you really can't fly that fast,"

"Yeah, I can. Watch," Kayli then stated, "Stand in the middle of the gym so I don't hit you," She then flew around the gym faster and faster until all Cathy saw was a blur. Kayli then let go of a scream when her clothes burst into flames, and she skidded on the gym floor for two hundred feet.

Cathy grabbed a towel, padded out the flames, then wrapped it around her and asked, "Are you alright,"

"Yeah, I'm okay, but I can't say that about my clothes,"

Cathy sat on the gym floor next to Kayli, looked in her eyes, and asked, "Since you are a Christian, why do you have a tattoo on your tush?"

Kayli sighed then stated, "I told Steve that I didn't want it, so he gave me a Mickey, and when I woke, I had a sore sit-down and that stupid teddy bear on it."

Cathy asked, "Can I ask you a personal question? What was your relationship with Steve,"

"Grose at times, but I managed,"

"Don't give me that I'm alright, young lady; I know what went on, so out with it,"

"I can handle what Steve did to me, so don't bug me with all kinds of questions,"

"No, you can't, and stop lying to yourself,"

Kayli put her hands on her hips, saying, "If you think I'm fibbing, then you tell me what happened between Steve and me,"

Cathy whispered a short prayer, then stated, "Steve disgraced and humiliated you every single day by calling you all kinds of derogatory names, having you walk around the house in something skimpy. But the worst part was when you had to sleep with Steve and caused an almost unbearable shame because of what he did to you every night. Now you locked it away inside of you, thinking that it will go away."

"Well, it will!" stated Kayli in defense.

"No, it won't because I've been in your shoes. Thor sent me on an undercover mission to find out what Wilford was doing. He caught me by surprise and dragged me to his place. Sorry to put it this way, but Wilford beat the living crap out of me, trying to get me to reveal Thor's plan. When I refused, Wilford did things to me that I was ashamed to talk about. He then slashed me multiple times about my body, then packed me in a wooden crate, and sent me back to Thor. It was only by the grace of God that I lived."

"You're just saying that to make me feel good," stated Kayli.

Cathy quickly glanced around to ensure no one was coming and opened her white blouse, revealing dozens of slash marks on her stomach, sides, and chest. She stated, "I was like you, trying to hold things in to deal with them on my own until Rose told me I could be healed emotionally through the finished work on the Cross of Christ."

Kayli's eyes filled with tears. She curled up in Cathy's lap and cried herself to sleep."

Thor walked into the gym, up to Cathy, and asked, "What's wrong with Kayli? Is she sick,"

Cathy stated, "What Steve did to Kayli was inhuman. I say we send somebody to Earth to rescue Steve from Area 51 and drag his sorry hide back here to face his crimes against this Gnomes. Then, hopefully, we can get him to talk,"

"Having Steve face his sentencing, I agree with you, but I don't think Steve will talk," stated Muncy.

Cathy smiled and said, "I have a program on the Three-dimensional Particle Acceleration System that will have Steve singing like a Canary."

Thor stared at Cathy, saying, "You still want to get back at Wilford for what he did to you some years ago,"

"Guilty as charged, Sir,"

"I'll call Moon Base 23 and have Calistus do the proper scans of Area 51 and draw up the necessary ID for you and Kayli,"

When Muncy heard Cathy and Kayli were going back to Earth after Steve, she demanded to go along.

Thor stated, "You and John can go only as backup."

On the beach of Smile Lake, Leprechaun Patrick O'Brien sat on Kayli's blue blanket and stared at her clad in her green one-piece bathing suit for a good minute, which gave the little Gnome the willies. She then shouted, "For crying out loud, Pattrick, will you stop staring at me,"

"Sorry, Lassie, I was wondering what is holding you together after all you've been through, and It's not sheer willpower." He then placed his hand on her stomach and pushed in a few places, then said, "Nope, Nothing in there."

A frustrated Kayli shouted, "If your wife ever saw you doing that to my tummy she'd slap you silly, and of course, I'm not pregnant. Now get off my back, will ya,"

Patrick stated, "Doc Patrick was just checking to make sure, stood, pointed to her heart, saying, "But there's something in there that should come out,"

At this time, Jed softly approached Kayli from behind and rubbed her neck. She spun around and shouted, "You!" and landed a hard right cross to his jaw. Then, he said, "That's for putting a bun in Darlene's oven, and we are no longer mates."

Patrick stated, "Lassie, there's a field of butterflies three miles south of here, why don't you check it out,"

With Kayli gone, Patrick stated, "Laddy, if you want to stay healthy, stay away from Kayli."

"Are you threatening me, Doc," muttered Jed.

"No, but you're messing around with the wrong Gnome."

"And what is that supposed to mean,"

"I'm on to you," stated Patrick and walked away,

About two days later, Thor handed Cathy and the others their papers and IDs, saying, "I want this mission at Area 51 to be a simple in-and-out job. John and Muncy, at the slightest sign of trouble, I want you two to jump in, wielding all the technology you can. Calistus and Su will be ready with a portal if needed,"

At the gate of Area 51, the guard carefully studied Cathy and Kayli and asked for their IDs.

The guard handed Cathy's ID back immediately, saying, "You're all set, Major Loganberry. About ten minutes later, he handed Kayli's ID back, saying, "You're all set, General,"

Kayli snapped, "Do you have a problem with me being General because of my size? Corporal?"

"No, Sir,"

Inside, when Cathy asked to see the alien, she was denied. Kayli marched up to the commanding officer and stated, "If we don't see the alien right away, heads will roll. Do I make myself clear,"

"Yes, Sir, right this way, Sir." shouted the officer.

At Steve's cell, Kayli stared at him, saying, "Ugly looking thing isn't he,"

Steve stated, "Hey, I'm not ugly,"

Cathy touched the guard's shoulder, saying, "Can you get me a glass of water?"

"Sorry, Sir, but I'm not allowed to leave my post,"

When Kayli distracted the guard, Cathy put him in a sleeper hold and opened the cell door. She then contacted Moon Base Twenty-three, saying, "I need a portal out of this dungeon, and I want it ten minutes ago,"

Calistus stated, "Because of the depth and the thick ceilings, the best I can do is give you a portal to somewhere in Utah."

"Anywhere is better than here. Now move it," stated Kayli.

Just then, an alarm sounded, and Cathy shouted, "Hey, Cal, it's gotta be now or never because we're about to have visitors,"

Cathy and Steve dove through the portal, but it closed too quickly, stranding Kayli. She tore off her top and flexed her wings, saying, "Nice meeting you, fellas, but it's time I took a powder," Then she flew over the men's heads and down the corridor until a metal door to the outside slammed shut. Kayli called upon her reserved strength and slammed her fist on the door, sending it flying.

Outside, Kayli sored sky word and was out of sight in a split second," She contacted Moon Base Twenty-three and asked, "Hey Calistus, where did you send Cathy and Steve,"

"Once Cathy and Steve were outside, I opened a portal to the Institute. But because I had to send the portal beam through all that cement and rock, then open a portal to the Institute, it shorted out the system and will be down for a week,"

"A week," shouted Kayli, "What am I going to do until then?"

Callistus quipped, "Sit on a rock and Twitter your thumbs,"

An irritated Kayli let go of a scream, then said, "Get me off this backward piece of rock right this minute! Do you hear me, Calistus?"

"I was pulling your wings, so calm down, Kayli; I'll have a portal opened in five minutes,"

12

Kayli on the run

At the Institute, Kayli approached a guard and asked, "Where are they holding Steve?"

The guard answered, "Steve T Rogers can't talk to anyone, Thor's orders."

"I wanna interrogate the prisoner; after all, I spent three months posing as his gal Friday, silently taking the garbage he threw at me."

The guard said, "Okay, he's on the second-floor cell room 5, but he is not allowed visitors,"

"Thanks," stated Kayli and rushed off.

On the second floor of the Institute Building, Kayli marched up to cell room 5 and shouted, "Hey, keep! Open this door before I kick it in,"

A tall man clad in a deep blue uniform stared down at the Gnome and said, "Big talk for a little thing like you. But Steve can't talk to anyone, Thor's orders,"

"I'm allowed to question him, so open this stupid door,"

"Sorry, no can do,"

Kayli screamed, "I said open this door before I give you a fat lip."

Rose approached the guard and asked, "What's with all the noise up here?"

The guard stated, "Little Miss Loudmouth is demanding me to open Steve's cell room door."

"Loudmouth." Shouted Kayli. "One more wrong word out of you, mister, and you're gonna need false teeth,"

Rose stated, "Calm down, Kayli, guard, open the door,"

As soon as the cell room door opened, Kayli flew in, grabbed Steve by his collar, and screamed at the top of her voice, "How dear you treat me like chattel, abusing me for your fleshly pleasure. Now I am going to take it out on your hide."

Rose tapped the Gnome's back, saying, "I think you should back away before things get out of hand,"

Kayli let Steve go, but as she turned to fly away, Steve grabbed her left arm and threw her against the wall. Then they said, "You heard she threatened to attack me, and I was just defending myself."

Kayli slowly stood, stared at Steve for a second, let go of a loud scream, flew, and slammed into Steve's chest, feet first, sending him flying backward five feet before landing on the floor. But before Kayli could do anything else, Rose picked her up by her waist, saying, "That's enough out of you, young lady."

Kicking and screaming, Kayli hollered, "Let me go so I can pound the snot out of that piece of work for what he did to me,"

Muncy approached Rose and said, "I'll talk to her,"

When Rose put Kayli down, she boulted back to Steve's cell room.

Muncy knelt in front of the Gnome, saying in a soft tone, "You are not going to solve things by beating the crap out of him. You need to forgive him and let Christ handle him."

Kayli hung her head, saying, "Yeah, I supposed you're right. Nobody loves me, everybody hates me, I might as well eat bugs," then giggled.

Muncy took Kayli into the cafeteria for an ice cream sundae and asked, "What do you know about Tiny Malone, Steve Thomson, The Twins, and Dunkin?"

Kayli popped the red cherry in her mouth and said, "Tiny Malone is a fanatic for horse Racing and has his thoroughbreds that he calls Comet, with hopes to make big money. Steve Thomson has a greenhouse that has plants from all over the galaxy. The Twins run a nightclub on HP 5 called The Lucky Star. Dunkin owns a string of cafes on Dicapl. But all of them like their women small, cute, and sexy like me, and trust me, I know."

Muncy inquired, "Do they use their business to smuggle drugs?"

"They sure do. Take Steve Thomson; He has these lavish planters with fake bottoms. Tiny hides the drugs in the stall, and the Twins and

Dunkin use the waitresses to pass the drugs. But the trick is to catch them because a lot of them are sneaky."

"When you are finished with your Sundae, come with me."

On the fifth floor of the Institute, Muncy turned to Cathy and asked, "Is the Three-dimensional Particle Acceleration Program ready to go."

"All set."

Muncy knelt and said to Kayli, "Take as much time in there as you want."

Cathy opened the door, and Kayli's eyes grew large; saying, "It's a virtual program of my home in the caves when I was a little thing. Thanks, Cathy."

"Enjoy," stated Cathy. She turned to Muncy and said, "Kayli told me about Big Tony and the others, but all of them together won't measure up to Steve's evilness. I know because I spoke to all of them. Tiny told me that if he had his way, he'd vaporize Steve for the way he treats Kayli."

Muncy glanced at her watch and said, "Steve's hearing is in two weeks, and I, for one, will be there,"

Thor approached Muncy and said, "Sam, Dora, Rose, and I are gonna visit the Twins nightclub on HP5, and we would like for you and John to join us to make six."

"Sure, but John can't make it, and I'll be packing my energy pistols."

Sam, a short, stout man with red hair dressed in black pants and a white shirt, escorted his wife Dora, a five-foot-tall woman in her fifties, clad in a floral blue dress. Thor was dressed in a black suit and tie, with Rose clad in a burgundy slack suit, and Muncy, in a fancy red dress, entered the Lucky Star Nightclub.

Dora glanced around and commented, "I bet he cornered the market on black paint and twinkling lights."

One of the Twins, Bart, approached Thor, shook his hand, saying, "This is indeed a pleasure having the Galaxy Sentinel in my club."

Thor stated, "We thought we mix business with pleasure,"

As Dora passed Bart on her way to their table, she said, "Very tacky if you want my opinion."

A waitress clad in a skimpy red French maid outfit approached their table and asked for their order.

Thor stated, "Just bring a pot of coffee and a container of milk, and we'll be all set."

"Just coffee?" asked the curious waitress, "Are you sure you don't want any drinks?"

"We're all teetotalers," stated Thor,

After the waitress left, Sam stated, "I don't think the twins you're gonna be stupid enough to pass drugs while we are here,"

"I just want to rattle the twin's cages, with hopes they'll make a stupid mistake,"

After an exotic floor show of scantily clad women, Kayli walked in and approached Bart, handed him a leather pouch full of drugs, saying, "Here's your weeks delivery,"

A nervous Bart whispered, "What are you doing? The big boss said that all drug deliveries are to be postponed until after The Galaxy Sentinel and his cohorts back off."

"But Steve is being held by Thor, so what are you talking about?"

"Not that halfwit, Steve, the real boss behind all this said to back off for a while. Now, where's my kiss?"

Kayli glanced at Thor, flew up and kissed Bart's lips, then said, "We'll get together at your place for some nooky later." and left.

A waiter approached Bart with a white tablecloth over his arm, bumped into him, excused himself, and then left.

Bart turned around and smiled sheepishly, saying, "Thor, old buddy, friend,"

Thor asked, "What's in the satchel?"

A nervous Bart stated, "I don't sell drugs; that dumb Sprite handed it to me to set me up."

Thor opened the satchel, then said, "Bart Walters, I arrest you for possession of an overabundance of chocolate bars."

Bart grabbed the satchel, reached in, and took out a handful of small chocolate bars. Patted Thor's back and said with a smile, "Better luck next time, Sentinel,"

In Bert's luxurious home in the country, Kayli was dressed in a thin lacy nightshirt. Met Bart at the door with a smile and handed him his evening martini.

He growled, "You stupid Sprite, you almost got me arrested this evening by handing me those drugs in front of The Galaxy Sentinel."

"I didn't know he was going to be there, and I didn't get the inner office memo that no drug delivery until things cooled down."

"You're my inside man at the Institute and supposed to know what's happening."

"Things are in lockdown since they caught Steve. Hey, you up for the evening meal? It's juicy pork chops, mashed potatoes, mushroom gravy, and corn."

"No thanks, I'm going to bed. You gonna join me, Sweety,"

"I'll be in as soon as I put the food away,"

Some twenty-two minutes later, Kayli walked into the bedroom with its plush white carpet and a dark brown blanket on a canopy bed. Kayli Tapped Bart on his face, sighed in relief and said, "Good, he's out like a light, thanks, Doc Chrissy, for the powdered sedative. Kayli then thought, *"After I put a pair of my undies in his bed to make him think we did something, I'll do some snooping,"*

Early the next day, Kayli entered Thor's office clad in jean shorts and a short-sleeve white shirt. Handed Thor the list of Bart's contacts and reported, "There is no such thing as the Twins. It's just Bart. The name The Twins is a ruse. One last thing: thank you, Sir, for suggesting I ask Doc Chrissy to give me a sedative to put in Bart's drink. So, I didn't have to get in bed with him."

Thor asked, "How are you holding up?"

"Better and not bitter about Jed. Oh, a Thor, Sir, this is just a gut feeling. I'd do a deep background check on Sprite Jed because he may not be as innocent as he puts on."

Thor then stated, "Jed, you can come in now,"

Jed somberly entered, stood aloof from Kayli, pointed to her, and said, "That Gnome can't be trusted."

Thor asked, "Do you have proof to back up your accusation?"

"She threatened to smush Darlene with a boulder if she got in her way. When I was trying to rescue Kayli in the desert, she attacked me and nearly tore off my clothes. I mean, she was a wild animal, and I had to sedate her just to keep her from killing me."

Thor stated, "It's hard to believe that a little thing like Kayli can wheel that much power."

Jed showed Thor a video of one of Kayli's workouts and said, "As you can see, she is a danger to the Institute and everyone who lives here."

Thor stared at the Gnome and asked, "What do you have to say, Kayli."

"I did threaten to smush Darlene because she stole my mate and I was upset."

"That's no reason to threaten someone with violence."

"What about the desert? Did you attack Jed?"

"Not that I can remember. He gave me something to put me out because of the severe heat prostration."

"Before I make a judgment, I want to speak to Muncy, John, Darlene Cathy, and a few others,"

Jed asked, "You're not going to lock her up?"

"Until I have more evidence, no. but I will restrict her,"

"Meaning," asked Jed.

"Kayli's been under a lot of stress here lately. A few weeks rest may be all she needs,"

Thor then said, "Sprite Darlene is pregnant, and it could very well be yours."

"Did Kayli tell you that? Did she? Well, it isn't true,"

"Sprite Darlene had her regular checkup that same day two got together."

"Well, it wasn't me, and that's all I will say,"

Kayli smiled, saying, "On that note, I'm leaving,"

Kayli took two steps and fell on her face. She stood, looked at her watch, and screamed, "You jerk! You tripped me and broke my watch,".

"It's not my fault if you're clumsy."

Kayli let go of a shriek and jumped on Jed, pounding his face with her fist.

Thor and two security men pulled the Gnome off a bloodied Jed kicking and screaming.

Jed stated, "Didn't I tell you she's dangerous to be around."

Doc Chrissy rushed into Thor's office, pulled down Kayli's shorts and underwear, and shot her with a sedative.

Some two hours later, Muncy greeted the Gnome strapped to the bed in the infirmary and said, "You've been taken off the case and will have to wear a monitoring bracelet. Which means any signs of anger it will put you out,"

Kayli stated, sobbing, "I've been framed by Jed, and Thor knows it."

"Oh, since you were out, Jed provided Thor with evidence that you are the kingpin behind the drug smugglings."

"That's a lie, and Thor knows it, so why is he siding with Jed?"

"Things will work out in your favor; just give it time,"

"Time my sit-down. Give me my clothes,"

"Can't because Thor has ordered full restraints to go with the monitoring bracelet," stated Muncy.

An angry Kayli ripped off the monitoring bracelet, broke the straps that held her to the bed, and stated, "I'm outta here," and flew out of the Institute building in her Jhonny coat.

Thor rushed into the infirmary and asked, "What happened?"

Muncy stated somberly, Kayli escaped, and don't expect her to be back any time soon,"

Thor stated, "Lock her house and post a twenty-four-hour guard just in case she comes back for her things. Then, send an alert to the police about Kayli. Muncy, you're taking her place,"

In the Institute's Galaxy Café in the housing project, Jed sat in a booth With Muncy and John and questioned, "Is it true Thor sent out an APB on Kayli?"

John took a swallow of his coffee and then asked, "Why are you happy about someone who was your close friend,"

"She was more of a pain than a friend,"

John inquired, "Not to be nosey, but why were you in a bar on HP-5 with Dunkin yesterday."

"Me, in a bar? Not on your life," stated Jed.

"A woman said she saw you coming out of a bar,"

"Well, that woman needs glasses because I've never been in a bar in my life."

Muncy stated, "That woman was me, and if you want a photo of you leaving the bar, I can show it to you."

"Oh, oh, now I remember, I went in the bar to use the men's room."

John did a scan of Jed's blood count, showed him the results on the scan, and asked, "Why is your blood count .02 if you weren't in the bar,"

Jed stated, "If I had a drink in the bar yesterday, my blood count would have returned to normal an hour later, so your scanner is busted,"

John stated, "That is true for humans, but you are a Sprite, and the alcohol Level in a Sprite's body takes 48 hours to return to normal,"

Jed smiled sheepishly, then said, "Hey, it's been nice chatting with you guys, but I've got to be going,"

After Jed left, Muncy stated, "Sprites are benevolent creatures with a childlike attitude, but Jed doesn't seem to fit in with the rest of the Sprites somehow."

John stated, "Find Kayli. She'll know why Jed doesn't act like a Sprite."

Under a lonely overpass on HP 5, Muncy took a foot-long silver rod hidden in her sleeve. Waved it over the cement wall of the overpass until it picked up a metal plate. She pushed it, and a door opened. Muncy rushed inside the dimly lit passageway to a rusty door and knocked.

Kayli opened the door clad in her Johnny coat, smiled, and said, "I pray you have something for me to wear."

13

Kaili's demise

Muncy handed Kayli some rags saying, "This is all I could scrounge up."

Kayli held them up saying, "You expect me to wear these cleaning rags? they're barely enough to cover what's needed,"

"You could sew up the back of your hospital gown and use it as a dress,"

Kayli stared at Muncy saying, "You're joking, please tell me you are joking."

Muncy opened the rusty door, picked up a brown paper Bag, handed it to Kayli saying, "I was just checking to see if you still had your sense of humor."

"Ha, ha, very funny, now tell me you brought me something to eat, and no more funny business."

Muncy displayed a weak smile then said, "Be right Back."

Muncy returned an hour later, handed Kayli a foot long sausage and pepper grinder and a thermos full of chamomile tea saying, "I would have been back sooner, but I ran into Jed,"

Kayli placed her food on a moldy piece of wood four teed long and three feet wide that was supported by four wooden crates, sat on one, then prayed over her food.

Muncy sat on an old wooden crates by the makeshift table and asked, "Why doesn't Jed act like the other Sprites,"

Jed is a Pigsise Sprite from the far side of the planet Belladonna and they consider themselves a higher class of Sprites and won't have anything to do with the rest of us."

"How did you meet Jed,"

"Before I worked for the Institute, I lived on Planet Haskel Prime and worked as an inner office messenger Gnome. I met Jed one day during the noon meal and we seem to hit it off right from the start. A starry eyed me could only see a hunk of a Sprite and didn't see the backstabbing weasel that he is. After we were mated, he vanished out of my life until he found me in the desert unconscious. He erected a tent with a humidifier that sprayed a mixture of exotic oils. Then rubbed some kind of a cream all over my body and lay me inside the tent without anything on still out cold. After the treatment we recommitted our relationship. But what puzzles me is Jed knew I was a Gnome and didn't dehydrate the way the Sprites do so there was no need for that treatment."

Muncy took her scanning wand, slowly waved it over Kayli then said, "Jed used the dehydration treatment to apply a new kind of tracking compound on your body. Jed recommitted his life to you to keep your mind off what he was really doing."

Kayli took a swallow of her tea and asked, "How do I get the tracking stuff off me?"

"Be right back," stated Muncy.

Some twenty minutes later, Muncy handed Kayli two pounds of caraSteve butter then said, "Smear this all over your body, then let it sit for an hour before washing it off. That should do the trick and make it snappy because Jed is trying to lock onto your position,"

Kayli smiled then said, "Then let's not disappoint him."

Muncy asked, "Kayli, what's seam is running around that little brain of yours?"

An hour later, Kayli was merrily strolling up a busy Avenue with Muncy. Spotted Jed approaching. Whispered to Muncy, "Follow my lead," She then purposely bumped into Jed. Then screamed, "You pervert! You grabbed my no, no zone. Officer, officer,"

In seconds, a police officer stood glaring down at Jed. Muncy stated, "Officer O'Brian that man bumped into my friend just so he could have his fleshly jollies,"

Jed hollered, "She's lying, I tell you she's lying,"

Officer O'Brian patted Kayli on her head saying, "A little thing like her lie? You're the one who's lying, now off to the hoosgow with you," and called for backup."

With Jed gone, Officer O'Brian picked up Kayli, put her on his left shoulder and asked, "How's my little daughter doing?"

Kayli put her arm around his head saying, "I'm ok now. Could you do a background check on Jed,"

"I thought you two were mates,"

"So did I until he left me, then when I found him years later, I caught him cheating on me," Kayli then whispered something in the Officer's ear. He smiled saying, "Consider it done, my we lady," and put Kayli down.

She took three steps, an energy blast struck her midsection, she screamed and vanished. All that was left of Kayli was black dust that blew away by a passing car. Officer O'Brian returned fire but the assailant was gone.

The next day the newspaper read, Gnome, Kayli Aubrette killed last night in a drive-by. She was a young energetic twenty-five year old Sprite and lived on the planet Pylee. The wake will be tomorrow at noon.

After the funeral, Thor sat at his desk listening to rise in crime due to the increase of drugs. Bowed his head and thought, *"I don't believe that Little Kayli was the head of the drug Lords."* He then sentenced Steve to life at the Institute, locked away from society. Thor then arrested Bart, Dunken, and the others for drug trafficking and things quieted down.

Behind a solid holographic rock wall in one of the caves on the Planet PX-12 in the Blue Ringed System. Jed was busy in his drug lab cooking up a new kind of drug that was more powerful than the last batch. In walked Kayli and bellowed, "Back at again I see!"

Jed quickly spun around and said, "I thought you were dead. Oh well. No more games, no more fooling around," Pointed his energy pistol at her and said, "Time to die love of my life."

Kayli said, "Before you turn me into micro dust. What happened to Lady Martha? The one who use to sell flowers on the corner of Park and Vine on Pylee?"

"She found out I was the King Pin behind the drugs being sold on the street. So, I took her to my place one night for the evening meal and killed her with one blast of this energy pistol."

"So, Greg, Steve, Bart and the others all took their orders from you,"

"For a Gnome, you're pretty smart too bad you Have to die."

Kayli smiled and said, "Did you get all that on video, Thor?"

Sam, Thor, and five of the Institute's security rushed in and arrested Jed on drug charges and several counts of murder.

Epilogue

Muncy returned to Wickenburg, Arizona, as a top agent of Earth's surveillance: Nicholas and his wife, Starlight moved back to HP5 and became the head of security there.

Thor gave Kayli Aubrette a medal for bravery and she proudly displayed it on a blue velvet in a fancy gold frame and hung it on her living room wall. Hoping her fellow Sprites would stop harassing her and show her some respect. But they teased her all the more. Calling Kayli, a fraud, cheat, and a liar, to the point that she could not go to work without being pelted with eggs by other Sprites. So, she quit her job on Sprite Security and was in the middle of packing when someone knocked on her door. She opened it, stared at Thor, and said, "Sorry, Sir, but I'm catching the next transport back to Pylee, where I can live in peace."

Thor stated, "There is going to be an assembly in the cafeteria in 10 minutes, and I want you there."

Kayli stated, "No, Sir, I am tired of being pelted with eggs."

"I'll put you on my shoulder,"

In the cafeteria, Thor congratulated everyone for a job well done and said there would be a considerable range in everyone's paycheck. After the cheers quieted it down, Thor brought Kayli to the front, stood her on a high pedestal, brought up Moonbeam, head of security, and announced, "Sprite Kayli is being promoted to second in command of security."

The cafeteria grew quiet as the Sprites, not knowing how to react, prayed Kayli wouldn't seek revenge.

The Mysterious Stranger

The Characters in the Story

Calistus
A human male who runs Moon Base 1. He is Thor's top agent and is employed by The Agency, started by Sam, Thor's friend.

Snow Wolf
This creature is nearly the size of a horse with long, bone-white, shaggy hair and has massive golden eyes with three-inch long fangs. One drop of its saliva will cause the body to swell until it explodes from the pressure. During that time, the victim gasped for air and is in extreme pain.

Su Wong
Human oriental woman with black hair from Earth. Who is 5'6" tall Calistus's wife and met him under a tree. She loves tea and crumpets and is a master in the martial arts.

Carla
A double agent who works for the Agency

Ken
An Agent out to kill Calistus and his wife

Johnson
A halfwit agent trying to kill Calistus and his wife

Admiral Sam the Stout
A friend of Thor at the Institute and the one who started the agency for mysterious strangers.

Thor

Or the Galaxy Sentinel is rugged looking. He works better alone and has a tough time working in a group unless he is the leader; he can accomplish more things when alone and can easily focus on a task set before him. Thor grew up on a farming planet and was more trouble than he was worth because of his powerful desire for adventure. His parents did everything they could to teach him farming, to no avail. When he reached nineteen years old, Sam took him under his wing and gave him a job working for the Agency on the planet Avalon Prime. He is now in charge of the Institute, hidden on a small planetoid in an undisclosed galaxy. Thor is an independent, self-willed individual and will put his life on the line when needed. Thor loves his coffee and can drink eight cups daily without thinking about it.

Cherry R. Blossom

was born on Planet Haskel Prime, which is slightly smaller than Earth. Cherry's younger sister was Jasmine, who disappeared and was presumed dead at sixteen. But she was found years later, on Earth. Cherry is a six-foot-tall, well-built woman with long, wavy brown hair who loves pastel colors and red lipstick. She is soft-spoken and gentle. She is the first one to give an encouraging and uplifting word to others.

General a male lion

He stands 5 feet tall from front paw to the tip of his ear. His first owner was McCarthy, who severely mistreated General and was sent to a tropical planet where Thor found Toby. He named him General because of his enormous size and overreaching roar. General is a kitten, despite his massive size, but he knows when criminals are nearby. One roar from him, and crooks freeze in their tracks. He works on the security staff at the Institute, helping to keep things under control. Thor and Cherry is alive today because of the General's keen sense of criminal activity.

Sam

He is short, about five feet three inches tall, and rather plump with red hair. He lives for the adventure; the more danger involved, the better he likes it and is also known as Admiral Sam the Stout.

Cecil

He lives on Pylee and is Captain of the Planetary Security Force.

A Prairie Mite

It's a dark gray ball resembling a dust bunny with eyes.

Admiral McCarthy

He runs the Agency and out for his gain.

The CEO of the Universal Exports

He worked with Admiral McCarthy to corrupt the Agency

The Deadly Whisperer

It is a five feet long pipe with a flared open at one end. At the other end, it's closed and rounded. There is a pad for the shoulder and a handle and trigger set up close to the pad. On top is a simple crosshair for sighting. It can turn a 5 story brick building into powder.

The Institute

The Institute sits atop Mount Baldwin some seven hundred feet above Smile Lake on a hidden planetoid in a asteroid field called the Rock Pile Two hundred fifty men and women guard and work at the Institute.

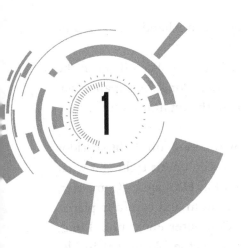

The Rescue

A tall, ominous-looking figure dressed in a flowing, dark blue cloak and wide-brimmed hat seemed almost to glide silently down a forbidding pitch-black street; pausing momentarily to scan the area, he crossed the boulevard that bordered the park. A police officer hollered, "You! Stop where you are!"

The stranger dashed across the street and into the park, with the officer in pursuit. The police officer quickly radioed for backup as the stranger ducked behind some concealing bushes in a shelter of darkness.

When the officer rushed past him, he dashed down a slight incline and across a narrow bridge that spanned a small stream. The stranger stopped momentarily, then went left along the stream until he noticed a wolf nearly the size of a horse with long, bone-white, shaggy hair. The massive golden-eyed beast turned, lowered its head, and growled, baring vicious three-inch fangs. With a powerful spring, it leaped forward a full thirty feet in the cloaked figure's direction and a sudden blast of energy from a swiftly drawn pistol struck the animal, liquefying its body and a bubbling, yellow-brown ooze seeped into the soil.

The stranger methodically checked the area to see if the wolf had attacked anyone. Noticing a human foot protruding from behind a large rock twenty feet away, he ran to the boulder to determine if the digits owner was alive. He gently lifted the young woman clad in tan slacks and white blouse and was about to return over the bridge when a voice halted his progress.

"Freeze! Put the woman down and place your hands behind your head."

The stranger quickly spun around, hitting the police officer in the face with the woman's foot. The stranger bolted along the stream, then abruptly turned left across the tennis court to the retaining wall, where he suddenly disappeared.

Once inside his abode, he sprinted down a long, dimly lit corridor into a spacious room with a huge concave screen on his right and what resembled an oversized easy chair in front of it. He stated, "Computer, light." Then rushed to the right rear of the room and carefully placed the woman on a hospital-style bed saying, "Computer, enclosure." Long, narrow doors flipped open. The stranger grabbed the folding wall inside. Pulling and shaping it until it had formed a ten-by-ten room. He then commanded, "Computer, "Snow Wolf antidote, twenty-five parts per million." A clear, half-round cover moved up from under the table, sealing the woman inside. She began to gasp for air as a light blue mist filled the chamber, and then she passed out. Ten minutes later, the cover flipped open, and the woman sat up and screamed, "Get back! You're that creep that everyone has been talking about."

She sprang off the bed and darted across the room, trying to escape. The stranger rolled his eyes, muttering, "I really don't have time for this." He took a short, thin rod from under his cloak and fired it at the fleeing woman. She flew forward several feet before sprawling face down on the floor. After she was placed back on the bed, a panel opened to reveal a med-droid, who promptly ministered to her lacerations.

Some four days later. The stranger entered the room and approached the woman's bed and said, "I almost lost you." and smiled benevolently.

Some two minutes later, your body parts would have been splattered throughout the room. The ointment the med-droid has applied to your wounds is healed."

The woman struggled fiercely against the straps that bound her securely to the bed, screaming, "Let me go! You are so in trouble, mister!"

The stranger informed, "Please, try to calm yourself and hear me out. I am Calistus, and I mean you no harm. You were attacked several days ago by a very deadly animal, called a Snow Wolf. One drop of its saliva will cause the body to swell until it explodes from the pressure. During that time, the victim gasped for air and in in extreme pain. If you will calm down, I will free you. However, you need to stay here for a week or so just to make sure you have fully recuperated. If you will follow me, I will show you to your apartment."

Calistus led the wary young lady to an archway across the large room from the entrance. Turned left, touched a small, round silver disk attached to the wall by the door. Upon entering, he turned right to a computer terminal attached to the wall, waist high. "First, you need to enter your name into the system, then step into the alcove just left of the terminal and press the green button. Then, return to the terminal, you will see a vast selection of clothes on the computer screen. After you have chosen your wardrobe, the clothes will appear on the shelf to your right."

As Calistus left, the woman spoke the name "Carla" to the computer. Barely ten minutes passed when he heard a horrendous shrill "You have got to be kidding me," coming from her apartment. He immediately rushed in and saw her standing in the middle of the floor, covered in a tent-sized mint-green garment. Verging on laughter, Calistus asked. "So, this is what pachyderms are wearing these days."

"Is this your idea of a joke? Look at this dress! It's at least a size fifty; you're right; an elephant could conceivably wear this."

Calistus chuckled, "Did you move while you were in the alcove?"

"Yes, why?"

"You're supposed to remain motionless while in the sizing alcove. Step back in and try it again; this time, don't so much as even breathe."

Fifteen minutes later, Carla emerged, wearing a form-fitting mint green outfit. She said, "Yesssss! Now that's a tad better. Can I keep the clothes?"

"Absolutely, you can help yourself to a few more outfits while you're at it." "By the way, I never caught your name."

"I never threw it. Anyway, it's Betty," Curious, Calistus asked, "Would you mind explaining why you entered' Carla' into the computer?"

"I'm still a bit nervous around you and had expected you to concoct some devious plot of some kind to destroy the world. Bear with me I just need a little more time."

"No problem. At any rate, this is the main room or control room. This overgrown chair, with its two enormous arms, is the command chair. The curved wall behind you is actually the computer screen."

Calistus pressed a small yellow button and said. "Computer, bring up an image of a Snow Wolf."

As the animal appeared on the screen, Carla gasped at the sight of the ravenous, silver canine with its ears flattened and lips curled into a snarl. He reassured her that it was merely a hologram.

Carla stated, "Don't mind me, but I don't care if it is only a three-dimensional picture; it still creeps me out."

Calistus accidentally hit the sound control, activating the audio file of the Snow Wolf's unearthly howl.

Carla instinctively jumped into Calistus's arms saying. "Will you give a person heads up when you're going to do something like that?"

"Get over yourself," Calistus curtly replied as he lowered Carla to the floor.

Calistus stated, "On the other side of the room, we have the snack counter; the room on the right is our medical facility."

Carla asked, "What counter? All I see is an empty corner."

Calistus walked to the far left corner and touched a round, blue metallic disc on the wall.

Carla stepped back surprise as a counter rose up from the floor and several cabinets slid down from the ceiling.

Calistus stepped behind the counter, as Carla found a stool to sit on. He then asked, "What flavor coffee would you like? Mine is favorite is Coconut-Hazelnut,"

"I'll have the same, please." Stated Carla. Hey, I know of a place in Kensington, Connecticut called the Kensington Café. It's a great place to eat."

"Connecticut, I've never heard of that planet before."

"Duh! It's a place on Earth. Apparently someone doesn't get out much."

Calistus strolled to the command chair and nodded towards the screen. and said, "Here is a look outside the base, enjoy the view."

Carla surveyed the stark, boulder-strewn landscape stretching in endless desolation and questioned "Don't you ever get lonely up here on the moon?" Calistus' answer was stone silence.

Just then, the video screen flashed and the admiral appeared. Calistus immediately saluted the superior officer. and asked, "Sir?" The admiral leaned forward and scowled, "Why haven't you caught the third Snow Wolf, yet?"

Calistus replied, "I lost its trail, but I hope to pick it up soon."

"I'll give you four days to capture it, or you'll be doing guard duty on a deserted planet."

The picture returned to the surface as Calistus scratched his head. "I don't have the slightest idea as to where that third wolf is. Every time I scan Earth, it comes up negative." He turned and was surprised to find Carla concealing herself in the corner and asked, "Why are you hiding? It's alright if the admiral sees you here."

Carla sipped her coffee and reluctantly pulled a memory crystal out of her purse saying, "I'm, ah, not a Tramp. I was told that you were messing up on all of your assignments, so HQ or Command ordered me to check up on you." Carla then hung her head sheepishly saying, "I was also instructed to make you look like a dolt, If I hadn't been attacked by that Snow Wolf, you'd be on a penal planet, right now. I did a background check on you while I was changing, then hacked into the Agency computer and discovered the truth. My father lied to me about you. Take the memory crystal and destroy it because the information on it about you is devastating."

Calistus screamed, "Your, father is the admiral?"

"Never mind that. Why do you let the Agency push you around, the way you do? You're the best agent they have. I've seen your file, and I know what you're capable of doing and there is no sane reason for the way they're treating you considering your rank." she continued, "And the years you have in the Agency, you can name the base you want to call yours, and they can't deny you! I'd be interested to see them transfer you to a mining colony. Ever since that McCarthy bozo took over, strange things have been happening."

Calistus admitted, "Am I supposed to take you seriously, after you've been deceiving me all along? You're going back to Earth right now."

Calistus grabbed Carla's arm and proceeded down the hallway to transport bay. Struggling, Carla yelled, "Stop! What do they have on you, that allows them to manipulate you?"

"Absolutely nothing, let's go."

"No, no, you're hiding something, what is it?" she asked.

"Al right, I guess an explanation is in order. You're nothing if not persistent,"

Calistus slowly made his way back to the control room. Head bowed, he solemnly intoned "Computer, activate imaging scanner, and zoom in on the Republic of China. Do a DNA scan for Su-Wong."

Within a few seconds, an image of a petite, oriental woman came into focus as she sat demurely under a tree with two cups of tea. Calistus turned to Carla, "That's the reason why I'm stuck here, on this barren rock. Several years ago, I took some leave time and went to Earth for a while. As I was sitting under a tree in China, enjoying the day, I heard someone ask, "Excuse me, sir. My feet are tired, along with the rest of me." I looked up, to behold a beautiful young woman, to real, but real she was, with a personality to match her looks. Obviously, I couldn't refuse her request. As she settled herself near me, she told me all about her family, and how her father sold paintings in the marketplace. I listened intently, since I couldn't get a word in. Quite the gabber, that young lady, But, then that's part of her appeal. After about fifteen minutes, she was asleep, head on my shoulder. Somewhere around dusk, she woke up, timidly thanked me for my shoulder and bid me good-bye. I asked, "Do you mind if I walk you home?" That started a trend, I'm happy to say. For the next three weeks, I forgot that I was an outsider, visiting Earth. Every day we'd meet under that same tree. She would always bring tea and something special to eat. How can you beat this: looks, mind and talent in the kitchen? One day, though, she was a no-show. I went to her home, only to find it abandoned. I had no choice but to return to Moon Base One, without knowing what had happened to her.

Settling in, I received an urgent transmission from the admiral. He informed me that I had violated the primary dictate of the Agency, and I was instructed not to see her ever again. If I did, they would kill her, because they couldn't afford the possibility of her discovering who I was. Fast forward, three years later, and she still comes every day and sits under that tree, waiting for me to arrive. The day I meet her again under that tree, is the day I condemn her to death."

Then an alarm abruptly went off and the screen switched to a map of the Canadian Rockies. Calistus threw on his cloak, and started for the exit, when Carla protested "Hey! What about me?"

Continuing his way back he asked, "What about you? The admiral's little spy stays here."

"Think again, mystery man. I can help you with Su-Wong. The Agency never advocated murdering innocent people. I don't care who my father is, this is going to stop now," she declared.

"Fine, anything to shut you up, grab your gear and let's go."

Carla then asked, "By the way, What's the deal with the cloak? Got a flair?"

"Yes and no, actually this cloak is the finest garment ever invented. If you touch your left collar, it activates the heating unit, keeping you nice and toasty. When you spread the cape around you and touch the brim of your hat in front, it turns on the camouflage shield. The new agents nixed the cape and broad brimmed hat because it looks rather archaic, they want a more modern style of clothing. Now, these idiots are paying the price for not being fashion plates, or trend setters most of the agents can't finish their mission because they're exposed, this is the result of poor training, bad judgment and cheap equipment.

Before we capture that beast, I need to make a call first." Calistus tapped in a code on the arm of the control chair, causing the screen to turn several shades of blue.

"Voice verification, please."

"Commander Calistus of Moon Base One, Earth. The screen cleared and a tall man, heroically proportioned with curly brown hair and an impeccably trimmed van dike answered, "Thor here. How can I assist you?"

Calistus replied, "Sir, we met several years ago in Posa City. You told me if I ever needed your assistance to contact you. As you know, I work for the Agency which is based in Posa City, the same organization you and Sam used to work for, years ago. There's something happening in the Agency, something that is completely against organization policy and by-laws. You may recall, I mentioned to you a lovely lady I met on Earth. I was instructed by my superiors to never have contact with her again or, she would be eliminated."

Thor interrupted, "Say no more friend, I'm on it. I'll get ahold of Sam."

Several minutes later, a heavyset man with a red beard and hair to match came into view. "What's the story with my alma mater?"

Calistus replied, "I won't bore you with the little details. He said in a nutshell; "They hired a new boss four years ago. Since then, headquarters has been hiring agents who are underqualified, and ill prepared. I have also been, told that if I make contact with my lady friend on Earth, again, they will kill her, in order to keep the Agency a secret."

An angry Sam roared, "Are you serious? If anyone even looks like they're about to attack your girlfriend, blast 'em!. You have my permission to do so. I ran the Agency for fifty years and we never harmed a soul. The next time you speak to the admiral, tell him Sam the Stout is coming to pay him a visit. Trust me, by the time I leave, things will be back to normal. Sam out."

The screen promptly returned to moon landscape.

Calistus beamed down to a remote area, high in the Canadian Rockies Scanning the surroundings, he said, "Carla, head in that direction, I'll go this way, maybe we can flush the big bad wolf out into the open."

Five hours later, Calistus decided on a well-deserved rest sat on a tree stump and waited for Carla to arrive. When she finally appeared, he smiled and asked, "See any signs of an extra-large puppy-dog roaming around these parts?" She shook her head, no, "Are you sure you have the right location? Maybe the computer messed up."

Calistus said nothing. Instead, he produced a foot long, black rod with a white tip, from under his cloak. Pressing the white end Carla's eyes widened, eyebrows raised in shock. "That's a forbidden device in the Agency. Anyone caught using one will be discharged and court-martialed, immediately."

"I'm fully aware of that fact, Carla. However, this handy little gadget will help us to locate this mythological pooch."

A little confused Carla asked, "Ummm, mythological pooch,?"

"A pack of Snow Wolves consisting of no more than two." He then explained, "Besides that, an animal that large should have left tracks of some kind, and we found nothing." Calistus waved the rod at arm's length in several semicircular motions then said, "Okay, due north about three yards."

He then pointed to a pile of brush. "Carla, see what's under there."

She cautiously uncovered an object that resembled two pie plates fused together. Hesitating for a moment, she asked, "What is this?"

Calistus answered, "A decoy. It emits false Snow Wolf signals. Toss it into the air, will you please?" One flawlessly aimed shot from his weapon vaporized the airborne disk.

Calistus put his arm on Carla's shoulder and said, "I want to show you something." He led her to a ridge overlooking a vast, shimmering lake, far below and said, "There is nothing like this in all the galaxy. Beings come here from as far as the Blue Ringed system, just to sit here, and be awed by the view."

The next thing they knew, someone pushed them and the two plummeted downward to the jagged protruding rocks. Barely fifty feet above the trees, Calistus activated his patch, sending them back to Moon Base One. Their two bodies hit the floor in the entryway, knocking the wind out of them. Calistus regained his footing and marched purposefully into the control room and said, "Computer, activate the three dimensional projectors, project a life-size Snow Wolf in a cage, add sound, and animate it." He marched over to the control chair, called the Agency and said, "Admiral, I have your so called third Snow Wolf, as you can see." The admiral frowned, as if in total disgusted.

"Calistus, you're a slacker, I'm not impressed. You should have captured that animal long ago. I want you to relinquish the Moon base and your position with the Agency. This organization needs individuals who can handle their assignments as ordered, with professionalism and expertise. And I might add, not just go off somewhere seeking out a one night stand."

2

The Come Back

Calistus lost his temper and said, "According to the rule book, chapter one, page three, paragraph two, it states that any agent who has over twenty years of service can claim a base for their own. Therefore, I claim Moon Base One, Earth, as mine. As of this moment, all the access codes have been changed. Furthermore, sir, I am bound for Earth to see Su-Wong. If anyone tries to stop me, it'll be their misfortune. One last thing, staring in hesitation, The former Admiral, Sam the Stout, is going to be paying you a visit."

The admiral then softly answered, "Maybe I was a bit hasty in asking for your resignation. The base is yours. I'll even throw in a new star cruiser."

Calistus smiled. "I figured you'd respond positively to my demands, sir." Satisfied with the admiral's reaction, Calistus ended the transmission then said,

"Now, to meet a lovely lady under a tree in China."

Carla questioned, "Aren't you afraid of what they might do to her?"

"Let them try; it'll be the last thing they'll ever do."

Calistus sat under a tree afar off and watched Su-Wong patiently waiting for him. His mind was clouded with questions: Will she forgive me for being gone for so long without telling her? What do I say to her? He slowly stood up and walked to where she sat and asked, "Mind if I sit down next to you? I could really use some rest."

Su-Wong turned suddenly to see Calistus standing before her and shouted, "You're back!" and leaped up into his arms saying, "I knew you'd return; it was a matter of when and never stopped believing."

Calistus leaned back against the tree and said, "Su-Wong, I don't know how to say this, but I'll try."

Su interrupted, "I know you aren't from Earth. I can also sense that you're in some sort of trouble. This time when you leave, take me with you. My parents are both gone now; You're all the family I have, all the family I need."

"How did you know I was an alien?"

"The last time we met, I followed you to let you know I wouldn't be there that next week. I was about to call you when you vanished into thin air. I slowly walked over to where you had disappeared and prayed you'd return soon. My prayers have been answered."

Calistus sat quietly drinking his tea, his eyes never wavering from Su and said, "Those weeks we spent together were like heaven to me. I would have given up everything just to be with you, but the Agency, the organization I now regret working for, informed me that if I saw you again, they'd kill you. Rather than risk your life, I stayed away. It tore me apart not to see you, but at least I knew you were safe. The only problem is you're not safe any longer."

"How can I not be safe as long as I'm with you? Please, let's just enjoy the moment."

Tell me about my pendant, the one my grandfather gave to me just before he died."

Su-Wong removed her oval pendant, made of a transparent material, and handed it to Calistus, who studied it intently for a few minutes then said, "These eight large dots, mixed with several small ones, are planets. This dot on the right side, which looks fuzzy, is a Sun. One dot that stands out more than the rest of them, with six dots scattered around it, is the main planet in the system; This is the Pylean solar system. The inscription on the bottom reads, 'My roots are in Pylee, my home world.' Your ancestors were from the planet Pylee; the pendant is made of crystalline, an indestructible material,"

Calistus took a deep breath and said, "I need to spirit you someplace, love, for obvious reasons; the sooner, the better."

"No! I am going with you! I'm not letting you out of my life again, now or ever."

"Listen, to me, you're thinking on emotion; you can't do that. Your safety is a priority one. You've got to let me take you to a place where you can't be found by agency assassins if such a place exists. It's the only way,"

Calistus helped Su-Wong to her feet; she spun around and threw her arms around Calistus's neck, and said, "Marry me."

Without warning, a blast of energy split the silence of the afternoon's silents. Startled, Su tripped over a tree root and fell to the ground. Calistus instantly covered her with his cloak to protect her. Seven more shots riddled the cloak as the two lay motionless on the ground.

Calistus whispered, "Don't move. As long as we stay under my cloak, it'll blend in with its surroundings."

The two lay on the grass for about five minutes before Calistus said, "I think we're safe now."

"I was wondering how long you two were going to lay there, pretending," a voice rang out.

Calistus quickly sat up with Su by his side and said, "Ken! What are you doing here?"

"The Admiral sent me here to kill Sue Wong. Hey, after I knock her off, want to talk over old times at the café just over the hill?"

"Let me understand this: you want to kill Su, then talk over old times with me as if extinguishing a life was nothing," Calistus asked.

"Look, buddy, nothing personal. You two stand on your feet. Calistus, move over by the tree; the last thing I want to do is hurt my friend."

Calistus looked down at the crystalline pendant in his hand and asked, "Mind if I put Su's pendant on her? It was a gift from her grandfather, and he told her to never take it off."

Ken shrugged, "Sure, go ahead, might as well go out in style."

Calistus gently fastened the pendant around her neck and whispered. "He can't hurt you," then backed away.

"As I said, Cal, nothing personal," Ken smiled as he shot Su.

The searing blast of yellow energy from Ken's gun formed a wall, a foot from Su, then immediately shot back and hit Ken, slamming him to the ground.

With surprising speed, Su sprang forward and kicked the gun away from Ken. She leaped into the air, her foot stopping an inch from his throat. Ken screamed, "Are you going to stand idly by while this Earthling kills your best friend?"

"Ken, you were going to kill the love of my life."

"You took an oath with the Agency to protect your fellow agent from harm."

Calistus yanked Ken to his feet, then pointed his gun in his face saying, "I know you were instructed to kill me after you vaporized Su."

"Wha, Cal, no! That's not true!"

Calistus showed Ken Su-Wong's pendant and explained that her ancestors were from the planet Pylee, which was part of the Planetary Alliance. Then said, "I happen to have an inside lead as to what is happening with the Agency, and it is going to stop."

Calistus and Su escorted Ken to an abandoned hut ten miles outside of town and bound him to a dusty old chair inside the hut. Su kissed Calistus saying, "I'll be back in a while."

A mystified Calistus stood silently watching her exit the hut. Within a half hour, Su entered the hut and tossed some clothes at Ken's feet and said. "Put them on,"

Ken grumbled as Calistus untied him. "You'll never get away with this. I'm talking to a dead man, Cal."

He grabbed the remainder of Ken's clothes and equipment, depositing them in a tidy pile on the dirt floor of the hut. He then placed the patch on top of the pile, activating it and sending Ken's clothes and equipment to the waiting vessel in orbit.

"Hey! Are you nuts? I needed that stuff! How will I return to the ship without my energy transport path?"

"Welcome to Earth, the backwater planet of the galaxy, as you call it. Enjoy your stay; you just may learn something, though I have my doubts."

Admiral Sam the Stout walked into the hut, and Calistus snapped to attention.

Sam just said, "Calistus, relax." He took one look at Ken and said, "Ken, the top man in the Agency. I've read your file, and I must say I'm very impressed with your achievements but I have a few questions. How can you be the top agent with only five years under your belt? Your file says that you single-handedly rounded up five wild grizzly bears on Earth.

Then, on the planet Avalon, you killed a three-ton Impact Beast. Just what is a three-ton Impact Beast?"

"Well, you see, sir, they are kind of hard to describe," Ken stammered.

Holding up his right hand in disgust, Sam cut him off. Ken. "The reason why it's hard to describe a three-ton Impact Beast is because no such animal exists! You are a pathological liar, a fraud; as of right now, you no longer work for The Agency."

"Wha, no longer work for, you can't do that!"

"Watch me! I founded the Agency, and I can do whatever I feel is right. You have two options: you can go back to Posa City and stand trial for scamming the organization or stay on Earth and work on developing a backbone."

"Wonderful! What about my wife and two kids? How are they going to survive without a regular income?"

Sam rolled his eyes and stated, "Another fabrication. I happen to know that you don't have a family of any kind."

Sam tossed a small bag of gold coins at the shocked agent saying, "Here, something to start a new life. Now get out of my sight, loser."

As the disgraced young man left, Sam turned to Calistus and said, "The admiral who is in charge of The Agency now is a devious individual. We need to do something to trick him into doing something stupid. Once he does, we'll have all the evidence we need to put him away for a long time. I think I know how to trap this ivory tower hoodlum. Oh, Agent Johnson was just sent to the planet Pylee to track down and capture alive, if possible, two escaped Thunderbirds."

Calistus answered, "Those birds are capable of carrying off a horse. Too bad one of them didn't get ahold of Johnson."

"I know what you mean. In any event, I want you to take over for Johnson on Pylee. Don't forget to take Su-Wong along because you'll need her help to complete the mission. I'll arrange a transport to pick both of you up at your moon base in twenty-four hours. You two can be married by stellar communications on Moon Base One; Carla will stay behind and watch things at the base while you're gone."

"What about the Admiral at the Agency? Won't he be furious when he finds out you contradicted his commands behind his back?"

"I'm counting on that poor excuse of an admiral to get so upset he'll slip up. That's when we nab him on charges. Now, if you read the fine print in the little green book you were given when you were hired, you'll notice that I still have the authority to supersede any order given by anyone. You two need to get moving so you can prepare for tomorrow's trip to Pylee, and if anyone even thinks of harming Su, by all means, let me know; it'll be the last thing they do."

Calistus held Su close to his side saying, "Hold on, we're going for a quick trip to the moon."

She looked up at him and said, "How can that be possible?"

As Calistus touched the transport patch on his shoulder, within a few seconds, they were standing at the entrance to the moon base.

"Welcome to Moon Base One, home of Calistus, the Defender of the Galaxy," he replied.

Carla greeted them sarcastically as Calistus and Su approached the main room, "About time you got back from gallivanting around the universe. When are you going to take out the garbage?"

A confused, Su asked, "Who is she, and what is she doing here?"

"I rescued her from a wild animal; she's recuperating. She doesn't live with me; she has her own space," answered Calistus.

Calistus showed Su-Wong around Moon Base One, then informed her that she would be sharing the underground apartment with Carla and instructed Carla to assist Su in choosing a new wardrobe from the computer. Assuming everything was under control, Calistus retired to his apartment until late that evening, when he went to the snack counter for a refreshing cup of hot coconut hazelnut coffee. As he was enjoying his drink, Su entered the apartment dressed in a bright red blouse with four-inch round yellow polka dots and a full white skirt with deep blue three-inch virtual stripes.

Calistus dropped his cup of coffee when he saw Su approach trying to keep from laughing so as not to hurt Su's feelings, he asked, "Who helped you become a fashion plate?"

"Carla told me that this is how your people dress. Do you like it?"

"Carla! I need to see you. Now!"

"Hmm, guess not," sighed Su.

Hearing no response, Calistus walked briskly to where Carla was and said, "I spoke to you, and I expect you to answer me. Why did you feel the need to dress Su up like some sort of circus clown?"

Carla swiveled the command chair around to face the annoyed Calistus and said, "She picked out the clothes herself. Don't go blaming me."

Calistus glanced at the floor, then riveted his gaze at her defiant smirk, cementing the fact that, in opinion, their relationship went beyond a mere personal clash and said, "I told you that that chair is not for your private use. The next time I catch you in it, I'll send you back to Posa City in chains," his voice, on the verge of shouting.

Carla paused momentarily and stared at Calistus, then regained her composure saying, "Whatever. I'm gonna crash. See you in the morning. Sorry about your precious throne," she quipped.

The following morning, as Calistus entered the main room, he noticed a door on the back wall, roughly three feet from the snack counter. He touched the silver disk on the wall next to the door, opening to an almost surreal scenario. There, floating four feet from the floor in a cloud of warm, pink mist, was Su-Wong, wrapped in a fluffy yellow towel and asked, "Where did this sauna come from," stammered Calistus.

"It was always here, but you never knew about it. Give me a few more minutes in this soothing mist, and I'll be good to go."

Suddenly, Carla marched up behind Calistus and said, "Computer, cancel antigravity and mineral mist. You're luxuriated enough, honey."

Su immediately fell to the floor of the steam room unfazed. She promptly rose, only slightly bruised and said, "I've had all I'm going to take from you, Carla. smiled and closed the door.

One minute later, Su emerged from the room and addressed Carla. "I am tired of your irreverent, sarcastic remarks and overall disregard and contempt for everything. You need a lesson in protocol."

"Oh, really? Is that a threat?"

"Take it any way you like."

Carla let out a hearty, condescending laugh then said, "Guess what, you slanted-eyed twit when I'm finished mopping the floor with your skinny little body, I'll let you use the steam room so you can take care of all the bruises I'm about to give you."

"Carla," Calistus yelled, "If you harm her,"

"Stand aside, Calistus, I need no protection," Su assured him. As if to prove her point, she leaped up and kicked Carla in the stomach, sending her flying backward several feet. Carla jumped to her feet and tried to land a right cross on Su's jaw. However, Su dodged and grabbed Carla's arm, hurling her to the floor. Su studied Carla's every move as she asked, "How did you fake your attack by the Snow Wolf?" A dazed Carla replied as she lunged forward at Su, "Excuse me? I didn't fake anything?"

Su leaped to one side, avoiding the attack and said, "After reading Calistus's report on the Snow Wolf and how he found you, I decided to do some investigation of my own. You were nowhere near the Snow Wolf since the scratch from one takes six weeks to completely heal. Explain how yours are already healed."

Su then leaped behind Carla and put her into a sleeper hold. Within a few seconds, Carla's body crumpled limply to the floor. Su turned her attention to Calistus and said, "You, husband of mine, have to learn how not to fall for the 'helpless female' act," her index finger waving inches from his face.

Calistus asked, "What do you mean?" realizing he had been used, a victim of feminine wiles. He silently cursed himself for being foolish enough to believe the wiles of Carla.

Su said "I am glad we had the marriage ceremony yesterday by way of that large video screen of yours. How do you think Ken knew about you visiting me on Earth so soon? Carla played the helpless female to throw you off track, and you played right into her arms."

Calistus had no reply, his head hung in sullen embarrassment.

As Sam arrived on the scene, he said, "Su's right. Carla was planted here to throw you off course. Anyway, are you two ready for your mission to Pylee?"

Regaining consciousness sooner than expected, Carla rose with renewed purpose and rushed toward Su-Wong. In a lightning move, Sam spun around and swung his fist, catching Carla's jaw. This time, the group reasoned, the treacherous agent would remain unconscious for quite some time.

Sam then addressed Calistus, "Don't worry about Moon Base One. I'll call Thor, who'll send me the help I need. Hey! Your transport vessel should arrive any minute, so hop to it, you two."

3

The Thunderbirds of Pylee

On the transport to the planet Pylee, Su asked Calistus, "Is there a place where we can see the stars?"

Calistus answered, "Follow me." He led her to the forward deck, and the two stepped into a large room with dimly lit lights and plenty of windows. They found a small table with two chairs by one of the forward windows. Calistus took Su's hand saying. "I'm sorry that there are no trees to sit under so we can drink our Tea. This place we'll have to do.

A waitress dressed as a French maid approached them asked, "Good evening. What would you like to drink?"

"Two cups of tea and two sweet rolls, please."

The waitress stared at Su in confusion and asked, "Tea? I'm not familiar with that drink."

Su reached down in her knapsack, pulled out a small green tin box, and opened it and asked, "Can you bring us two cups of hot water and two sweet rolls, please," she asked the waitress.

Calistus asked Su, "Have you ever worked for a company like the Agency before?"

"No."

"Then. Listen carefully because I'll only say this once. On a mission, you are not to fraternize with the locals at all. Most of your tracking will be done at night. If you can't neutralize the animal, it has to be destroyed to protect the citizens of the planet to which you're assigned. You will wear a wide-brimmed hat and a long, dark blue cloak. Above all, do not allow yourself to be distracted from your mission. Your cloak has a heating unit in it to keep you warm on cold days. It can absorb several direct energy blasts before the cape loses its ability to protect you. The cape also has a protective shield that will blend in with the surrounding area and render you practically invisible. Last of all, the cape is waterproof so that you won't get soaked to the bone during downpours."

"Who came up with all those rules and the cape we must wear?"

"Admiral Sam the Stout is the founder of the Agency, and he has proven the wide-brimmed hat and cape to be extremely effective. Oh, and the protective field is activated by touching the brim of your hat. In other words, you need the hat and cape for total protection."

"How is it that agents like Johnson don't wear a cape and hat?"

"The fault lies with the new Admiral; he's purchasing cheaper and flimsier equipment, thus endangering the agents' lives. Additionally, other things are going on that I can't discuss now. Regarding our first mission together, once we're on the planet, we need to locate the general area where the birds are, and then we'll camp in the woods until nightfall."

Wondering where their hot water and rolls were, Su called to the waitress, "Excuse me, could we get some service here?"

The lounge was strangely silent as Calistus approached the counter to inquire about their order. When no one responded, he slammed his fist on the counter several times hollering, "Service, please? Is this a morgue or a restaurant?"

He mumbled to himself, "That's it. I'm going in that kitchen and giving them a piece of my mind," He entered the kitchen only to discover it was devoid of anyone. Perplexed, Calistus exited the kitchen and grabbed his backpack. Once they were out of the lounge, he instructed Su to check the aft compartments for signs of life; he would go forward and attempt to talk to the captain. Fifteen minutes later, Su returned to Calistus, relaying she could not find a soul aboard.

"That's the least of our problems, Su. When everyone had left, the captain programmed the self-destruct to go off in twenty minutes. That was seventeen minutes ago. Leaving would definitely be in our best interest."

"What about contacting Admiral Sam?"

"We can't; the radio's smashed, but I do have an idea; there are two spacesuits that were somehow overlooked. Fortunately, We can use them to escape the ship's blast and hope that someone comes along to save us."

As the two propelled themselves away from the spaceship, Calistus reiterated, "We have to get as far from the ship as possible for obvious reasons. Each suit comes equipped with a thruster pack; as you leave the ship, push the blue button to activate it. Don't worry; I activated my personal homing beacon, so Sam should pick it up on the screen back at Moon Base One."

Seconds later, the ship exploded, the backlash and concussive aftermath hauling them for miles through the black void of space. Calistus and Su drifted unconscious for hours until they bumped into a fifteen-foot sphere.

Startled awake, Calistus proclaimed, "Hey! A life pod! Su, wake up!" 3

"Ooh, how long were we out," Su asked groggily.

"Who cares? The main thing is we're here. Calistus eagerly pried open the door to the life-saving pod. Once inside, Su quickly shed her space suit saying, "We never did get to have our tea and sweet rolls."

Calistus replied, "Give me a minute or two to find our location and then engage the thruster. Then we can concern ourselves with the past."

For the next two hours, Calistus tried to calm Su Wong's concerns in regard to being stranded in space. Suddenly, a constant beeping emanated from the control panel just above the hatchway.

Su nervously asked, "Trouble?"

"Possible."

"meaning?"

"The planet Pylee is coming up on our left, and we should be landing within the hour. Think you can stand the wide open spaces of planetary life instead of this claustrophobic little pod?"

Calistus tapped the life pod's landing control panel saying, "Stupid life pods drive me nuts; they never work right. Hold onto something; we're in for a rough landing."

Su immediately wrapped her arms around his waist and asked, "Umm, Calistus, how rough is rough?"

"Ever curled up inside a truck tire, then had someone roll you down a hill? Comparatively speaking. That's what it's like. The life pod will most likely hit the ground on a twenty-three-degree angle, bounce, and roll for a mile or so before it stops."

Calistus hurriedly secured Su and himself in order to brace themselves for what promised to be, in his description, a rough landing.

Flaming from the velocity of re-entry, the life pod struck the Earth on a twenty-degree angle, then bounced slightly, rolling crazily for nearly a mile across the open land, finally coming to a stop in a small stream.

Silence reigned briefly then Calistus asked, "Su, are you alright,"

"Ooooh, whoa. As soon as everything stops spinning, I'll let you know."

As the pair attempted to stand, the hatchway revealed a tall, lanky man with tousled blond hair and asked, "Are you two okay?"

"I think so," Calistus answered.

The man helped them out of the pod and leaned them against a large boulder.

And asked, "What happened?"

"The transport vessel we are traveling in had a glitch of some sort and exploded. My wife and I climbed into that pod and abandoned the ship, along with everyone else. As for the others who jumped ship before us, we haven't a clue."

"Would you two like to stay with me and my wife? I only live a mile or two from here."

Calistus took hold of his knapsack and said, "Thanks for the offer, but my wife and I will be camping out here for the night before moving on in the morning."

Smiling, the weathered gentleman extended his hand in friendship saying, "My name is Cecil. If you ever need me, I'm just over that ridge," he said with an unaffected friendliness.

Before Cecil left, he removed his hat and remarked as he squinted up into the sky, "There, up there. The thieving' varmint that's been stealing my animals."

Su and Calistus looked skyward and saw a bird, with a fifteen-foot wingspan power diving straight for them.

Calistus shoiuted, "Get behind the rock," then pulled out his photon pistol and fired a ten-second volley at the bird continuing its rapid descent.

Unfazed by the barrage, the avian's intent seemed assured. Calistus, however, was determined that such would not be the case. He fired again, striking the bird's breast. With a piercing shriek, it faltered, then dropped to the earth, dead before it hit the ground.

Cecil commented, "Nice shooting, stranger. I've been trying for months to waste that thing."

"This charmer is a Thunderbird, and somehow, it found its way to this planet. Oh, by the way, you'll never find a more delectable meal. If you don't mind, I'm going to carve off some of its breasts for dinner tonight. The rest is yours, bon apptit," beamed Calistus."

Cecil exclaimed, "Thanks, mister! This bad boy will feed my family for a month!" His face suddenly lost its glow and said. "Sir, if you could do my family and everyone in the village a favor? Stop that marauding idiot that's been trying to kill the Thunderbirds?"

"Consider it done. Now let's carve up that flying house for your family. Sorry, I should've introduced myself earlier. I'm Calistus, and this is my wife, Su."

Later, Su was finishing the last of her meat when Calistus remarked, "Sorry, your first space flight had to end up in disaster. I was hoping for a nice, quiet trip to this planet, where we could shoot a couple of birds before returning home to Moon Base One."

"The trip was interesting, I must admit, parts of it scared the life out of me. I wouldn't want to repeat the experience."

Calistus asked, "Would you like to spend the night in the life pod instead of out here under the stars?"

"I'll take my chances out here under the stars as long as you sleep with me. But aren't we going to search for the other Thunderbird and agent Johnson tonight?"

"No, I thought we'd rest a little before we went to work. Around dusk tomorrow, I think we should be able to locate Agent Johnson."

"How can you be that sure you'll find him?"

"Most of the agents who have been hired lately stay in the local hotels. As I mentioned earlier, this is wrong. We are to have as little contact with the locals as possible. Hence the name, 'Mysterious Stranger,' a name of which I've been extremely proud of all these years. Enough of that, it's been a long day, so let's get some sleep. Tomorrow, we'll have another long day because we need to plan our strategy on how to trap the last Thunderbird."

"Can't we just walk up to it and shoot it?"

Calistus remained silent as he doused the campfire to catch some much-needed sleep. He awoke around noon to a throbbing headache. Instinctively reached for his wife, only to discover she was gone. In her place was a note that read, "If you are as smart as they say you are, you should be able to find your wife before the big pigeon does. Regards, Agent Johnson."

"Regards. As if this is some sort of game," Calistus hissed. Johnson, like most people, understands one thing, and I'll accommodate him."

Just then, Cecil arrived in a six-wheel buggy and said, "I'll overstate the obvious: I suppose you're looking for your wife. That low life stunned both of you while you were sleeping, then drove southward. I think he's planning to use your wife as bait to capture the last Thunderbird."

"I see. And, how do you know all this?"

"Actually, I stood guard all night to make sure nothing would happen to my guests."

"Then you should have seen him sneaking up and abducting my wife. Why didn't you stop him?"

Sheepishly, Cecil hung his head and said, "He stunned me before I had a chance to react. Hop in; the cliffs are ten miles south of here and should be able to make it in time."

As the vessel knifed through the air, the serene, rolling grassland quickly morphed into a vast fissure, some three thousand miles long, fifteen miles wide, and three miles deep.

Su was strung by her hands between two wooden poles mere inches from the fissure's edge, with Agent Johnson concealed behind four massive boulders. Upon seeing Calistus approaching, he swiftly reacted and fired a lethal bolt of energy.

Narrowly dodging the volley, Calistus pushed Cecil out of the buggy and onto the ground. The two crouched behind the stalled buggy as Agent Johnson continued his deadly barrage.

Abruptly, several loud, eerie shrieks echoed through the vast canyon as the female Thunderbird began its power dive toward Su. Calistus. took the thin rod out from under his cloak, pressed a small button, and fired.

A blast of energy burst from the rod and struck the bird, causing it to veer from its intended course.

Agent Johnson pressed his assault, focusing his attention on Calistus' destruction.

"Stay here," Calistus instructed Cecil, "I'm taking that dirtbag out. His flowing cloak deflected Johnson's blast; Calistus casually approached the stunned agent and yanked the gun from his hand. While Cecil freed Su from her bonds, Calistus' eyes blazed with ferocity, and he grabbed Johnson by the collar saying, "I ought to string you up the way you did, my wife, and let the birds pick at your flesh, you sadistic, contemptible punk."

Cecil interrupted. "Cal, I know how you must feel now, but I can have our law enforcement here in no time. Trust me, we have ways of dealing with people like him."

Verging on panic, Johnson cried out, "Calistus! You can't let them lock me up! I'm an agent!"

"Johnson, shut up, you disgust me. By order of Admiral Sam the Stout, you are no longer an agent and get used to that sinking feeling."

Cecil produced a small round, blue, and white patch and adhered it to the back of Agent Johnson's neck saying, "That'll take care of him until I can lock him up. I'm also Captain of the Planetary Security Force, and that is a neural paralyzing patch. I've been looking for a chance to arrest this turkey for months. Everyone on the force has been walking on eggs, afraid to arrest him because of what he represented. Now that you fired him from his job, I can do my job."

Calistus answered, "We who work for the Agency are not supposed to interact with the population of the planet. We are to finish our mission and leave unseen, unnoticed. The situation with Johnson is not over yet; Admiral McCarthy, head of the Agency, will try to have Johnson released on a technicality. What I want you to do is entangle agent Johnson in your legal system, so much so that it will take a month of Sundays to file the paperwork to visit him once. If it comes down to putting him in a cell and forgetting he's there, do it. I do not want Johnson free, no matter what McCarthy says. Charge Johnson with every law he has broken, no matter how trivial. I don't care if it's jaywalking."

"You can count on me. By the time I'm finished with Johnson, he'll be doing three life sentences at hard labor, one after the other, with no chance of parole." "If McCarthy gives you a hard time, contact Sam at Moon Base One. He'll take care of all of your problems."

Cecil departed with Agent Johnson unceremoniously stuffed in the rear of the vehicle, bound for the holding cell.

Calistus and his wife traveled west along the ridge for nearly three hours until they came upon a fallen tree. He sat on the sprawling log overlooking the canyon, his wife beside him.

Su asked softly, "What are we looking for?"

"The Thunderbird should be gracing us with its presence sometime soon, I figure; that overgrown turkey dinner has made its nest on top of that high mesa out there in the middle of nowhere. If not, we search some more tomorrow and keep searching until we've covered all three thousand miles of this ditch."

"Would it be better if we activated the cape's camouflage so the bird wouldn't see us? Just a suggestion."

"And a good one. Oh! By the way, Su, I want to congratulate you on your courage when you were strung up for bird bait earlier."

"Courage? No, faith. I knew you'd come." Su's expression suddenly changed from one of serene warmth to concern. "Do we have to kill this animal? Is there a way of putting it to sleep, then transporting it back to its home world?" Y'know, that's one of the main reasons I married you. There's enough compassion in you to equal an army. Anyway, I may be able to come up with a solution to save Mama." Calistus then rummaged through his knapsack and managed to locate a small dart gun, along with several yellow darts and said, "Just what the doctor ordered, a dart gun with four strong sleeping darts."

"Umm, Cal, I hope they're really strong because the bird is coming straight for us,"

Calistus and Su rolled off the back of the log. As the Thunderbird passed them, Calistus quickly turned and fired his dart gun, striking the bird in the back.

The enormous avian convulsed, then spiraled downward, plowing into the ground.

Visibly satisfied, Calistus contacted Admiral Sam at Moon Base One via a tiny transmitter and said "Bird Man calling the nest, the Thunderbirds of Pylee are taken care of; unfortunately, one had to be destroyed, and the other is waiting to be transported back to its home planet. Agent Johnson is in Pyleean jail, serving three life sentences. One of the charges was using my wife as bait to try and capture the last Thunderbird. I'm happy to report that it failed, with the assistance of Cecil, Captain of the Planetary Security Force."

Sam replied, "Good job. Now, for your next assignment, I want you two to remain there and find out who was behind putting those birds there. Oh, and please inform your wife that she is now a full-fledged agent."

4

Pressure Point

During the pre-dawn hours, two shadowy figures moved down a deserted city street, silently entering the back door of the sheriff's office. As they approached the prisoner holding area, an incarcerated Agent Johnson shouted, "Calistus! What are you doing here?"

"Never mind that I need to ask you some questions. Who brought the Thunderbirds to Pylee?"

"It obviously wasn't you, Johnson, because leadership isn't one of your strong points."

Agent Johnson smirked, "I love you, too, Cal. He extended his hand through the bars of his cell in friendship to Calistus. Johnson then let forth a sinister laugh as a miniscule dart shot from a hidden gun in Johnson's sleeve, sticking Su.

She gasped, eyes rolled back, and collapsed to the floor. A panicked Calistus hollered, "Medic!"

Cecil immediately rushed in. "Good Lord, what happened?"

Agent Johnson casually replied, "Admiral McCarthy ordered Su to be killed and I was just following orders."

"Johnson, you're history." thundered Calistus.

Johnson merely smiled. "Wishful thinking. I'm protected by Pylean law. They have to keep me alive until I'm transferred back to Avalon Prime for trial. Of course, when Admiral McCarthy finds out, I'll be free in no time."

Just before the medics took Su away, Cecil remarked, "Your wife is very fortunate; indeed, the dart narrowly missed her aorta. She'll remain in the hospital for a while, but she'll recover." Cecil rested his hand on Calistus's shoulder saying. "Johnson's right, son, we have to protect him at all cost, no matter what he's done. Of course, if someone accidentally dropped the keys to the jail cell, and you were to find them, I couldn't do a thing about it."

Cecil slowly walked out of the holding area and, with a backward glance, dropped the keys on the floor. Calistus retrieved the keys to Johnson's cell saying, "Any last words before you depart this life?"

"Cal, are you deaf and stupid? You heard what your buddy said! You can't touch me because I'm protected!"

Calistus grabbed Johnson's right arm, breaking it so that he was prevented from further utilizing the tiny, concealed dart gun.

Johnson hollered, "Gaaaaahh! Are you insane? M-my arm,"

Calistus then slammed Johnson up against the cell wall saying, "My wife, Su, is a full-fledged agent by order of Admiral Sam the Stout. You, late friend, are dead." then he injected Johnson with a slow poison that was hidden in his cape.

"Wha, what did you do?"

"I injected you with a toxin that will stay dormant, unnoticeable, until you eat food, and it will then act as a catalyst to kill you. Now, why were the Thunderbirds brought here, and who is Admiral McCarthy working for?"

"If I tell you, he'll kill me."

"Then, we've got a bit of a double-edged sword here, don't we? If you don't tell me what I want to know, the poison will kill you, or I will. Any way you look at this, you're dead. Oh, and one more thing: the poison, if untreated, will slowly turn your blood into a liquid polymer. Bye for now and have a great lunch. If you're still alive tomorrow, when I return and have the information I want, then I'll give you the agent to neutralize the poison."

Calistus left Johnson's cell, withdrew the needle containing the poison and dropped it on the floor. He then took a short, thin rod out from under his cloak and fired it at the needle, vaporizing it.

The distressed agent asked, "Why did you do that?"

"To destroy all evidence of the poison. Thus, I'm the only one who can save you," Calistus said with a steady glint in his eyes.

Calistus vanished quickly and silently out the back door, leaving Agent Johnson to deal with his own fears. Approximately thirty minutes later, a mysterious figure clad in a long, blue cloak, dark glasses, and wide-brimmed hat that concealed his face purposely strode down the hospital hallway, then into a private room. The inhabitant looked up, startled.

"Cal," Su exclaimed, did you get any information from Johnson?"

"No, at least not yet. He'll talk; it's just a matter of when."

"So, what did you do to him? Knowing you, you most likely planted some dreaded virus in him to watch him squirm."

"Ha! Do you know me or what? I told Johnson that I had injected him with an undetectable poison. By the way, when are they going to release you?"

"They didn't say. I overheard a doctor tell a nurse to cook up some excuse to keep me here because they've never seen someone like me before I've fully recovered from my injury, though."

Calistus opened her locker saying, "Good, consider yourself released. Get dressed, and let's go. Once you have your cape and hat on, activate the camouflage field, so we can walk out of here unseen."

Late that evening, huddled around a campfire, Calistus and Su were painstakingly piecing together the scant information they had to try and determine who Admiral McCarthy was working for. Yielding nothing after two hours of frustration, they had decided to wait until after they questioned Agent Johnson again to conclude. Su was humming a tune as she made coffee when Calistus motioned to her not to move but to look down at her feet. There, by her left foot, was a small, charcoal gray sphere resembling a dust bunny, its two golden eyes fixed on her. Startled, Su jumped back saying. "Good Lord! What is that?"

Calistus calmly sipped his coffee then said. "It's a Prairie Mite. Legend has it they bring good luck when they wander into your camp. Legend aside, they're utterly harmless, just curious and benevolent."

"I hope you're right because it looks like he brought the whole neighborhood. Over there to your right, there must be a dozen of them."

Calistus glanced to his right. Two dozen glowing, little eyes were indeed peering at him from the darkness and said, "Su, hum that song again. I think they're music fans."

"Let's get some sleep. don't worry about the Prairie Mites; they will protect us." "Balls of dust will protect us?"

"Mm-hm. If there's danger near, they let out a screech loud enough to wake a cemetery's inhabitants."

Early the next morning, Su whispered, "Guess who slept with me all night?"

"You mean besides me?"

Su rolled her eyes and pointed. Snuggled next to her head was a Prairie Mite.

"I have an idea, Calistus remarked. "If he is around this evening when we visit Johnson, I'd like to take our new pal, the Prairie Mite, with us."

"Uh-oh. What are your plans for Johnson now?"

"I wonder if anyone has heard of a Prairie Mite with rabies?"

"So, what do we do until we set this 'deadly' ball of fuzz on Johnson?"

"Plan our next move. If Johnson doesn't talk, we still need to find out who McCarthy works for."

"What makes you think McCarthy is working for someone? Maybe he's just a greedy individual."

"You have a point. However, who's supplying him with the animals that he's using to terrorize the planets with? Hang on a second. Do you have a flair for the theatrics? As in, can you act like you're dying after being bit by a 'ferocious' Prairie Mite?"

Su giggled. "No problem. I'll use some toothpaste, so I look like I'm foaming at the mouth."

Later that evening, two figures entered into the holding cell where Johnson was incarcerated and Calistus asked, "Well, Johnson, ready to talk?"

"I'll take my chances with the poison you injected in me."

At that moment, Su reached into her knapsack and pulled out her pet Prairie Mite saying, "Hey, how did you get into my knapsack," she asked with mock surprise. "Ow! Hey, it bit me," Su suddenly fell to the floor, shaking and foaming at the mouth.

The Prairie Mite landed at Agent Johnson's feet and Calistus said, "The thing has rabies. Don't let it get near you, or you'll suffer the same fate as my wife." He knelt and tended to his suffering wife while trying to keep a straight face then said, "Back up in the corner of the cell. Now, are you going to tell me what I want to know?"

"Yes! Yes! Just get that thing away from me before it bites me too." Johnson shouted. As he plastered himself against the wall.

Calistus asked, "Who ordered you to put the Thunderbirds on Pylee, and who is McCarthy working for?"

"McCarthy's the top man; he's working with Universal Exports too. Universal Exports smuggles a dangerous animals onto a planet, and Admiral McCarthy makes a deal with the planetary government to get rid of the beast for some serious money. Now kill this thing, will you please!"

Calistus smiled as he picked up the Prairie Mite and put it on his shoulder so it wouldn't be trampled. At the same time, Su jumped to her feet and wiped her mouth then said, "Gotcha Johnson." She told the astonished agent.

"Who! What is this? What's coming off here?"

"If more agents were as dumb as you, the Agency would be in serious trouble. It was easy to trick you into revealing your boss's name."

Cecil entered the holding cell area at that moment. "Johnson and said, "I just finished talking to the judge on the planet Avalon Prime. He said that McCarthy wanted you to be transferred to Avalon Prime for trial."

Johnson interrupted and shouted, "Yes! I'm outta here."

"Not so fast. I told the judge, "Request Denied." Agent Johnson broke our laws, and it will be our courts that try him."

Johnson's elated, overconfident smile quickly faded as the anguished expression of one who faces a harsh reality.

Cecil opened the cell door for Calistus and his wife. Calistus handed the keys back to Cecil and said, "You dropped these." He then walked back into Johnson's cell and said, "This is for trying to kill my wife." Calistus then quickly spun around and stepped towards Johnson, landing a devastating right cross on Johnson's jaw, propelling him across the cell and into the bunk.

"Nice one, son. I'll take over from here; you two leave before anyone else comes," reminded Cecil.

"Much obliged, Cecil. You know where we are if you need us."

Before Cecil had a chance to reply, Calistus and Su were gone.

As the sun peeked above the horizon, Calistus contacted Sam at Moon Base One and said, "Mission accomplished, One bird dead, and one on its way home. Check Universal Exports; I believe they're working with Admiral McCarthy to swindle money out of numerous planetary governing systems. I'm uploading my full report to you now. And we'll wait for further instructions."

"Great work, Calistus," Sam replied. "You and your wife need to lay low for a while. Obviously, Admiral McCarthy is none too pleased over your success; He's declared open season on the both of you. This means that every agent in the Agency will be trying to waste you two. I don't need to remind you to do whatever you need to do to stay alive."

"Things are just beginning to get interesting, sir. Just in case we don't make it back, make sure McCarthy doesn't see too many more sunrises."

"You have my word that McCarthy and everyone connected with him will pay dearly for all the lives they took."

"Sir? Lives? I don't understand."

"I found out that McCarthy didn't retire the previous agents; he had them killed, so be careful. This is what we're dealing with. A real piece of work."

"There's only one place where we'll have a fighting chance, and that's in the Grave," answered Calistus.

Sam agreed, "It's rough down there, but knowing your reputation, it'll be a walk in the park. Take care of yourself and your wife. I'm counting on making you the head of all this when it's over, so don't disappoint me. Sam out,"

5

The Deadly Whisperer

Su looked at her husband with concerned and asked, "What do you mean by the Grave? Does it mean what I think it means?"

"No, but we might as well be dead. Come with me, I'll show you."

He led Su to the edge of the expansive canyon and said, "There's our destination; this fissure is three thousand miles long, fifteen miles wide, and three miles deep. With boulders the size of houses, mammoth caves, and rugged terrain, it is almost impossible to traverse. Many have ventured down there; very few have returned."

"Very uplifting. We are going down there because?"

"The organization we work for is called the Agency, remember, and it employs over three dozen agents, who are scattered throughout the galaxy. Admiral McCarthy has put a price on our heads because we pose a threat to him. In a short while, this place will be crawling with agents, all wanting to cash in on the money. By going down into the Grave, we level the playing field because only a few agents will try and follow us there, and when they do, we will be ready for them. One last thing: I grew up down there, in the Grave and I know this place, inside and out."

"How are we going to get down to the bottom of the canyon?"

"We're going to jump, so strap on your antigravity belt. Let's go before we're overrun with greedy agents wanting to profit from our deaths."

Suddenly a voice shattered the moment. "Calistus, you're slipping! I thought it would be much harder to catch you than this. I see you're still wearing that useless, stupid-overlooking cape and hat."

When they turned around, they were greeted by five agents leveling their energy pistols at them.

Calistus stated, "So, do you tin soldiers expect us to go along with you and your cohorts back to Avalon Prime without any resistance? The moment our backs are turned, you'll betray us the way you did other agents. The time is coming when you all will have to answer for your allegiance to McCarthy."

Agent Smith answered, "You might as well come with us; you have nowhere to run. The canyon is behind you, and the five of us are in front of you."

Calistus withdrew his short, thin rod out from under his cloak and fired several shots at the agents. Taking advantage of the element of surprise, he grabbed his wife and hurled her over the cliff. Su screamed as she and Calistus plunged to the jagged rocks below.

In midair, Calistus maneuvered himself to his wife and held her close as he activated his antigravity belt. With seconds to spare, their descent slowed, and they both floated safely to the bottom.

Once she stopped shaking, Su voiced her opinion, "You scared me half to death! Next time, give me the benefit of a warning when you're going to pull a crazy stunt like that."

Calistus replied, "Sorry, Love. Had to act fast before they shot us where we were."

"We should be safe down here, uhh, shouldn't we?"

"For the moment, though, we do need to be moving to my place up in the canyon. If those agents want to claim their money, they must produce our bodies."

Calistus and Su moved around boulders and tall, jagged spiral rock formations along a swiftly flowing river and on the bank grew bright purple mushroom balls.

Captivated by their benign, almost mystical appearance, Su stopped to admire them when Calistus advised, "Don't touch them; they're deadly. If you inhale the spores, they will lodge inside your nose, throat, and lungs, where they'll quickly grow and suffocate you. However, believe it or not, I think we can use them. There's a narrow passageway up ahead where we can set a trap for our unwanted friends. Down here, it's definitely going to be survival of the fittest."

"And how are we supposed to survive without food? We left it all up there." "Don't forget, this is my old stomping ground. There's food here that no one else knows about."

"Whoa, No grubs, worms, or freshly steamed beetles, I'm talking real food." "What's wrong with steamed beetles for dinner?"

"Do I really need to elaborate on that?"

Calistus chuckled as he pushed a rock on the canyon wall. The stone slowly opened to reveal a hidden cave and a rustic log cabin.

"Su, welcome to my home away from home. Dinner tonight will feature baked chicken, mashed potatoes, and gravy, with corn on the cob. For dessert, deep dish apple pie."

"This is great, but where did you get all this normal, actual food, and how did you get it down here?"

"I have my own power supply and food storage. The walls, floor, and ceiling are made out of a synthetic material that can withstand falling rocks from the cave ceiling. The food storage is a crystalline cube by way of my computer. Whatever type of food I need to preserve first goes through a process where it is broken down, digitized, and then stored in the cube, ready for use when needed. Oh, and I should add our master bedroom is back here. Speaking of which."

Calistus proceeded to open the bedroom door and got the desired reaction as Su gasped at the lavish bedroom before her. On the left side of the room was a colonial, queen-size canopy bed with a Tiffany lamp. Adorning the colonial nightstand. The floor was covered with a blue, soft, high-pile rug. On the far side of the room was a balcony, reminiscent of an elaborate, early twentieth-century movie place.

"This whole thing," Cal Su said, "Is beyond description. The view of the lake is absolutely breathtaking." Su sighed as she ascended the balcony.

Calistus stated, "The lake isn't real; it's just a backdrop I had someone design for me."

"I don't care if it's faux or not; I love it. How long did it take you to do all of this?"

"I threw it together in my spare time, which I had a lot of back then. Now, how about some dinner? You relax while I fix a meal fit for a queen."

Shortly after dinner, Su asked, "What is that noise I hear?"

Calistus walked to the right side of the living room, opened a panel, and pressed a silver button. Two long, thin, white rods moved slowly down from the ceiling, and a picture of the surrounding area outside appeared between them, revealing that several agents had camped just outside the door.

"What do we do now? Are we stuck here until they leave?" questioned Su.

"No problem. I'll give them something to think about."

He then opened a panel on the arm of the couch and pushed a red button. Fifty feet above, between rocks across from the secret entrance, an energy beam burst forth, grazing the left leg of an agents.

"It came from over there, let's go." Shouted Smith.

Calistus sat down beside his wife saying "I have twelve energy rifles hidden around the area, all set to go off at different intervals once they're activated. That should keep these clowns occupied for some time. And if they're foolish enough to break in the door, I have a high-powered rifle poised and set on rapid fire. If that doesn't work, the Deadly Whisperer can take out an entire army with one shot. So don't worry, we're well protected. On that note, let's go to bed, we'll deal with the tin soldiers tomorrow."

As the dawn's first rays of sunlight illuminated the bedroom, Su stirred in response. *"Aaahh, the smell of freshly brewed coffee, Blueberry pancakes, and bacon,"* she thought, not quite able to determine if she was dreaming of breakfast or actually smelling it. "How long have you been up," She asked drowsily.

"For a couple of hours. We can't fight on an empty stomach, so eat up. We leave in one hour. And yes, they're still camped by our front door."

"How do we get out?"

"The back door,"

As Calistus entered the bedroom, he touched the upper left-hand corner of a full-length mirror. It gradually moved back and flipped upward. Breaking into view was a pitch-black passageway.

"Well, Su, ready to tackle the bad guys?"

"Bring 'em on," she answered, "And, what's that you mentioned about a Deadly Whisperer?"

Calistus closed the passageway door and switched on a string of dimly lit lights. Attached to the back of the door was a five-foot-long pipe, flared open at one end, closed, and rounded on the opposite end. There was a pad for the shoulder and a handle and trigger set up close to the pad. The top featured a simple crosshair sighting.

Calistus was practically giddy when he said, "Observe, my dear, The Deadly Whisperer. This baby makes hardly any noise when fired. Its sheer destructive power is the mind-boggling force."

Calistus and Su warily made their way through the dimly lit tunnel for several hundred yards when the tunnel made a curve upward and to the right. At the end of the tunnel, Calistus pushed a rock on the cave wall to his right, opening a massive stone doorway high above the canyon floor. He pointed to their right and said, "The agents should be over there by those tall monoliths. Stand back, Su; I'm going to give these losers a lesson they'll have nightmares about for years to come."

Calistus positioned the whisper on his shoulder and fired. A faint whoosh and three massive rock pillars suddenly exploded into clouds of dust and tiny rocks that showered the agents below. Calistus fired two more times, nearly burying the agents with pulverized rock.

As he closed the rock door to the cave, Calistus pressed an odd-shaped rock on the opposite wall, opening another passageway.

"Hm. seems you were a busy little bugger when you lived here," Su commented dearly.

"What we need to do is to isolate Agent Smith from the rest of the group. Any ideas?"

"Actually, yes. You can use me as bait! I'll sneak around and get his attention so he'll follow me. When he does, you come up behind him and knock him out."

Su carefully made her way around several large boulders to where the group of agents were camped. When Agent Smith was alone, she emerged from behind a boulder and waved at him. Smith immediately sprang to his feet and followed her. He fired two shots, nearly hitting her. As Smith ran towards her area, he discovered Su standing next to a massive rock formation, her back facing him.

"Su Wong! Freeze," You're coming with me, dead or alive."

Su leisurely turned around and said, "The name is Mrs. Calistus if you please, and I'm not going with you; you're coming with me."

"You've been out in the sun too long, sweetheart."

"And you're deceiving yourself but it's nap time for you, buddy-boy," Su declared.

As if on cue, Calistus cautiously stepped out of the cave and fired his short, thin rod, stunning Agent Smith into unconsciousness.

"Su, grab his feet and activate your antigravity belt. Once we're back up top, there'll be a spaceship ready to transport us to Avalon Prime."

Once at the summit, they started towards the spaceship with their captive in tow. Suddenly, a sturdy, six-foot-three-inch gentleman exited from the ship and silently motioned them to stay where they were, Su and Calistus didn't argue.

The man took a dozen steps away from the vessel and gazed intently at the landscape in all directions, then fired his weapon five times in succession at the ground several hundred yards away. Smoke drifted up from the spots where he had shot the ground as if he had hit his target. He then signaled for Calistus and his wife to bring their captive into the ship.

"I'm Thor, and this is my wife, Cherry. You can stash your friend back there for the time being. Don't worry about the big kitty, that's General, our security lion. He'll make sure he doesn't bail."

Curiosity got the better of Calistus and asked, "Why did you shoot at the ground because there's nothing out there."

"That's the way it looks, I'll admit. Come, I'll show you what I was firing at."

Calistus followed Thor to one particular area in question. Thor bent down and lifted a patch of grass, where a sniper had dug a hole in the ground and was waiting for Calistus and Su to arrive and be assassinated. The sniper's chance never came. His lifeless eyes stared vacantly, just below the hole in his head.

"Incredible. I never would have seen that coming, Su and I would have walked right into it, for sure. Thanks, friend, I owe you one."

Once inside the spaceship, an intimidated Calistus came face to face with General, quietly guarding the doorway to Agent Smith's quarters.

"That is one huge animal. Wherever did you find him? Aren't you afraid he'll turn on you?"

Thor answered as he rubbed the lion's mane, "Nope. He's one big, lovable kitty, except when it comes to crooks, he's their worst nightmare."

Simultaneously, Agent Smith regained consciousness and demanded his freedom.

In answer to Smith's outburst, General sprang to his feet, spun around, and let go a bloodcurdling roar. The color immediately drained from Smith's face as the lion placed his mammoth paw on Smith's chest.

Thor grinned impishly. "General, you already had your dinner; we need him alive. Okay, Smith, I'm in the mood for conversation. Who's the man behind the swindle? Is it Admiral McCarthy?"

"I don't have the slightest idea what you are talking about."

"Mm-hm, if that's how you want to play it, General, he's all yours. Just don't leave too much of a mess."

Thor casually rose from his chair and entered the rear compartment. General was poised to crush Agent Smith's head with one bear trap bite when Thor said, "General, heel."

The lion immediately obeyed and padded only a few feet away from Smith, turned, and faced him, growling ominously, waiting for Smith to make a move.

"Ready to spill your guts, or do you want me to leave you with General again," Thor questioned the shaking perspiring agent.

"No! Please, no! I'll talk! Admiral McCarthy is the brains behind it all. Skimming money out of the planetary governments was just the beginning. He plans to maneuver all the governments to do his bidding, complete subjection, or he'll let loose even bigger creatures in their cities than those birds."

"Smith, are you remotely aware of how many innocent people will be needlessly killed because of this man's sick lust for power? Are you proud to have been a party to all this?"

Smith replied, "It'll be their own fault; they only have to obey him. Genocide can be easily avoided. Don't you understand?"

Thor's blood began to boil in reaction to Smith's warped reasoning and said, "You obviously blur the difference between right and wrong, Smith."

Thor grabbed Smith's collar, bunching up the area surrounding his throat to the point of suffocation and said, "There's no point in even trying to talk fact or logic to you. But I will tell you this: if we fail to stop McCarthy's plans, ponder the fact that you, in your boundless ignorance and blind servitude to this maniac, will have been integral in the extermination of hundreds of thousands of a planet's inhabitants. I, frankly, wouldn't want to live with your conscience."

The Galaxy Sentinel disgustedly threw Smith against the wall and, without a backward glance at the agent, exited the room.

"Cherry! Fire up Star Fire Two, and let's head for Avalon Prime before I've gotta concentrate on something else; if I keep thinking about this Smith idiot, I'll walk back into his room and vaporize him."

"Ready for takeoff. If you'll come up here and man the controls, I'll make some coffee for our guest. Hopefully, that'll occupy your mind for a while."

Moments later, Cherry served Calistus and Su their coffee. "So, how long have you been working for The Agency?" Calistus replied, "I started working just after Admiral Sam the Stout handed the company over to Commodore David, who suddenly took sick and had to relinquish the controls to Admiral McCarthy, his close advisor and things have been going downhill ever since."

"Time to buckle up, folks," Thor advised. "Destination, Avalon Prime's only minutes away."

Every onlooker's attention was averted to Thor, Cherry, Calistus, and Su as they escorted Agent Smith down Posa City's main thoroughfare toward the Agency building. Upon viewing General following close behind, many of the citizenry ducked inside nearby buildings for fear of their lives.

The Agency building itself was a massive, one-story crystalline structure. In front of the building is a beaux-arts-inspired fountain, surrounded by statues of animals throughout the galaxy. Admiral Sam met them inside the valued ceiling lobby. "McCarthy's office is down this hallway to our left."

As they entered the office, McCarthy's secretary explained, "I'm sorry, sir, the admiral isn't seeing anyone; you'll have to come back tomorrow."

Sam replied, "He'll see me now, whether he likes it or not."

"But, but, sir, you can't."

"Ignoring the secretary's protest, Sam stormed into McCarthy's office, leaving General and the others outside.

"And just what is the meaning of this," McCarthy shouted. The office door closed, cutting off the rest of the conversation.

General jumped onto the startled secretary's desk and made himself comfortable, causing her to fall backward in her chair. Before the surprised young woman could rise. General leaped off the desk to where the secretary was to ensure she was alright. He then began to lick her face, then curled up alongside her. She was beginning to hyperventilate, at a loss for words.

"It's okay, hon, believe me. You couldn't have found a better friend." Stated Cherry.

An agitated McCarthy abruptly hollered over the intercom, "Anne, call the police, now!"

Upon hearing his voice, General instantly sprang to his feet and began to roar. Sam was fortunate to be standing off to one side as the lion burst through McCarthy's office door shattering it like cardboard and stopped.

Upon spotting McCarthy on the opposite side of his desk, General lowered his head, face contorted in a snarl, and slowly moved around the desk towards McCarthy as if stalking his prey.

A wide-eyed, McCarthy softly said, "Good boy, Toby, good boy."

General discharged another thunderous roar and swatted McCarthy across his abdomen. Blood spurted from the wound as McCarthy fell to the floor, writhing in pain.

"No, Toby, No!" shouted a frightened McCarthy.

The enraged lion's mammoth paw slammed into McCarthy's body, tearing through his uniform and into his chest.

Sam and Thor desperately shouted in unison for General to heel to no avail. The snarling brut, enveloped in a white-hot paroxysm of animal rage, continued to furiously attack McCarthy. A minute later, the pleading, screaming, tearing, and roaring abruptly halted. General's demeanor swiftly morphed into quiet curiosity, playfully batting the shredded remains several times as if he were looking for a response. There was none. General turned away and curled up in a corner of the office and began to lick his paws, satisfied with what he had accomplished.

For the next thirty seconds, Thor and Sam gazed down at McCarthy's mangled remains and Sam aske, "Why did he continually call General, Toby?"

The secretary slowly entered the office, glanced at McCarthy's tattered body, and quickly turned away. Silence reigned until the woman explained, "About five years ago, a lion named Toby was given to McCarthy as a gift. Back then, I was his gal Friday and would go to McCarthy's residence late in the afternoon and find Toby lying restrained with a huge, thick chain, forced to sit in the boiling hot sun with no food or water. There were times when the poor beast could hardly move because of the beatings McCarthy gave him. I firmly believe McCarthy took sadistic pleasure in seeing Toby suffer. To say he was mistreated and abused is an understatement and there was nothing I could do to help him. She lifted General's massive head, placed it on her lap, and scratched behind the lion's ears. "No more abuse, Toby. Never again."

General rolled on his back as the compassionate young woman gently stroked the lion's chin.

The tearful secretary looked up at Thor and Sam and said, "By the way, my name is Anne. To continue what I was saying, I had arrived early one day to make sure the house was secure while McCarthy was away. I found Toby in the backyard tied up in the hot sun, as always. However, this time, he was half-dead from a particularly savage beating he had received from McCarthy. I had reached a decision this inhumane treatment had to stop. Somehow, I managed to move Toby inside the basement, where it was cool. During the next week, I nursed him back to health. When I felt he was strong enough, I contacted a friend to transport him to a jungle planet where he'd be safe from any further abuse from McCarthy, from anyone."

"That's where Cherry and I found Toby err, General, on a jungle planet. Well, apparently, Anne, he remembers, not only who was unkind to him but who wasn't."

"Animals aren't stupid, Thor," she replied, "They remember."

At that point, the CEO of Universal Exports entered the office and gasped as he saw the bloody carnage and asked, "Who's responsible for this? It doesn't matter because you'll never get away with this, any of you, not if I can help it."

Calistus grabbed the CEO from behind, slamming him up against the wall saying, "Shut your mouth. One false move, and you'll be joining McCarthy."

"I'd better close the place up before we have any more unexpected visitors," Sam said.

Thor entered the Institute's code into the video phone and said, "Rock, send a cleanup crew here on the double, we also need to fake McCarthy's death and devise a way to dispose of his body, errr, make that body parts. And no, I'm not trying to be funny. You'll understand once you get here."

"Whatever you say, Thor. We'll be there in a few minutes."

Thor turned to the CEO. "Terry Barons, heir to the famous Mister Barons meat pies. You're nothing but a petty thug hiding behind the law."

A belligerent Barons stated, "And you're just a superhero wannabe, sucking the life out of the system."

"Mm-hm, ramble on, buddy. When you were fifteen, you were arrested five times for breaking and entering and never did the time. During the next ten years, you were accused of bilking money out of several companies, but there wasn't enough evidence to convict you. You married a millionaire named Misty Pennyworth at the age of thirty. She mysteriously disappeared a week later, leaving you everything. A year later, you married Terry Williams, who also vanished while you were on vacation in the Blue Ringed System. Finally, you became partners in the Universal Exports Company, and after a year, your partners either vanished or signed the company over to you. Seems you've had an interesting life."

"Where did you get that information from? How, how did,"

With his arms folded across his chest Thor leaned against the intricately carved mahogany desk in the office and asked, "Ever heard of a place called The Institute, and a person called The Galaxy Sentinel?"

"What about it? That's just a legend and there is no fact to back it up."

"I've never considered myself a legend," laughed Thor.

Barons grew silent. His eyes widened with the grim realization that his life was about to take a decided turn for the worse. With rapidly failing bravado, Barons regaled, "I don't care who you are; none of it will stand up in a court of law. And if you harm me in any way, half the planet will be pounding on your door."

"I'm not impressed with your little tirade, Barons. Listen up, when I am finished with you, no one will come looking for you because everyone will think you are dead. Your lifestyle has testified against you, exposed you, and found you guilty, worthy of retrieval. Technically, Barons, from this moment forward, you don't exist. Society will never mourn your passing. You have been retrieved, taken out of society, never to return."

"I demand to see my lawyer."

A somber Cherry took hold of Terry's left arm as she disappeared with Thor and Barons in a flash of pale blue light. Seconds later, Rock appeared in the same manner as the cleaning crew. Two men deposited McCarthy's remains in a body bag and promptly vanished, while three women began the unenviable task of cleaning up General's handiwork.

Sam strolled back into the office after locking up and said, "Calistus, how would you like to take McCarthy's place?"

"Thanks, but no thanks, sir. I belong in the field."

"I see. Then, how would you like to train the new agents?"

"Yes, absolutely, sir, if it's out on assignment. This way, the new recruits can get hands-on training on what and what not to do."

Sam stared at Sue and asked, "Just curious, can you handle yourself in a physical confrontation?"

Suddenly, Agent Smith attempted to escape and Catlike, Su sprang forward and landed on top of Smith. Shaking her off, he jumped to his feet and tried to kick Su in the stomach. She rolled away, then flipped in midair, landing on her feet. Then, with one well-placed powerful blow to his chest, Agent Smith suddenly gasped and fell to the floor, dead."

"Well," Sam commented, "There's my answer, my kind of gal."

He playfully rubbed General's snout, "Come on, kitten, time we were moving along."

Anne the secretary, approached Sam and said, "Pardon me, sir, I've worked for both McCarthy and Commodore David, and I know more about running this Agency than the two of them put together. Well, what I'm trying to say is, do you think the Agency is ready for a woman commanding the troops?"

Sam paused for a moment then said, "Sure, why not? Don't worry about any legal matters concerning Terry and McCarthy's sudden disappearance. They'll be explained in tomorrow's newspaper."

"Ummm, sir," Calistus questioned, "With your permission, now that everything is over, is it possible for my wife and I to have a honeymoon? After all, we were married on the fly."

"Definitely, you've earned it. Go ahead, take a month off. By the time you return. You might have to attend another wedding."

"Sir? Who's?"

"Mine, I've had my eye on Dora, head of housekeeping at the Institute, for some time now. Just before I left for this mission, she agreed to marry me."

"Whoa! Never thought I'd see the day that the Great Admiral Sam the Stout went soft."

"Who's going soft?" bellowed Sam, "I'm in better shape now than I ever was."

Su then chimed in. "You really have to lay off those donuts, you don't want to have that tux tailored too much."

"Get outta here, you two, before I change my mind."

Epilogue

Su and Calistus were relaxing in the midday sun at a resort on the planet Dicapl. "What is this," exclaimed Su. The Galaxy Gazette claims Admiral McCarthy and the CEO of Universal Exports died today when their private spacecraft malfunctioned and was caught in the gravitational pull of the Blue Ringed planetary system's sun.

Su lowered the paper, perplexed and said, "Didn't that gigantic lion mutilate McCarthy in his office? The article says differently. Maybe we should call the paper and let them know of their error. Or is this yellow journalism?"

Calistus took hold of Su's hand saying, "The law has its checks and balances. The Galaxy Sentinel is the unseen hand of the law for those who manipulate the law for their own evil designs. He works secretly with the law, removing people like Terry Barons. Thor captures and incarcerates those who would destroy civilization as we know it. As a result, the Institute and its methods have to remain a secret. Sam, Rock, and what they do has to be kept secret also."

Su replied, "Thor, who? All I know is people should take better care of their private spacecraft."

Printed in the United States
by Baker & Taylor Publisher Services